TeensTalk

TeensTalk

**Real Stories
about Real Teens**

Malka Katzman

Copyright © 2014 by Israel Bookshop Publications

ISBN 978-1-60091-341-9

All rights reserved. No part of this book may be reproduced or transmitted in any form or by any means (electronic, photocopying, recording or otherwise) without prior permission of the publisher.

To contact the author with your story, or if you are interested in having a writing mentor, please email md@netnaki.net.il.

Published by:
Israel Bookshop Publications
501 Prospect Street / Lakewood, NJ 08701
Tel: (732) 901-3009 / Fax: (732) 901-4012
www.israelbookshoppublications.com / info@israelbookshoppublications.com

Printed in Canada

Distributed in Israel by:
Shanky's
Petach Tikva 16
Jerusalem
972-2-538-6936

Distributed in Europe by:
Lehmanns
Unit E Viking Industrial Park
Rolling Mill Road,
Jarrow , Tyne & Wear NE32 3DP
44-191-430-0333

Distributed in Australia by:
Gold's Book and Gift Company
3- 13 William Street
Balaclava 3183
613-9527-8775

Distributed in South Africa by:
Kollel Bookshop
Northfield Centre
17 Northfield Avenue
Glenhazel 2192
27-11-440-6679

Acknowledgments

This work is the product of Hashem's kindness. He granted me innumerable gifts, and some of them are the ability to write this book and the wonderful people in my life who've offered invaluable support.

To my parents, in-laws, siblings, and last but not least, my husband and children, thank you for everything that you mean to me, and especially, for cheering me on as this project took wings.

I thank my school teachers, wherever they may be now, for laying the strong foundations of *Yiddishkeit* in my life. This is a debt that can never be repaid.

I thank my childhood friends, some of whom wave from the pages of my story, for being the most endearing characters in the play of my childhood and teenage-hood. Although I don't have the privilege of speaking often enough to all of you, know that you remain friends to cherish forever.

Thank you, Chayala, for being a true friend.

I thank *Mishpacha* magazine, and especially Mrs. Daniela Thaler, editor of the *Teen Pages*, where some of the stories in this book first appeared.

To the whole staff at Israel Bookshop, and especially Mrs. Liron Delmar, I appreciate your efforts to make this book the best it could be.

Thank you Mrs. Malkie Gendelman for your expert editing and for the pleasure of working with you, and to Mrs. Chana Shweky and Mrs. Rochelle Gemal for your meticulous proofreading.

Mrs. Elisheva Appel has created a cover design I could have never even envisioned. Thank you for giving this book a new and creative dimension.

Thank you to the delightful teens who shared their beautiful stories with me.

And thank you, dear reader, for taking the journey of challenge, joy, and inspiration with me. I hope the stories in this book will touch you as they've touched me.

Contents

Preface: Dream On 9

On the Move 15

Be My Pal 101

Brains 111

The Guidance Counselor 116

Hearty and Healthy 121

Secrets 133

Backstage 145

Sink or Swim 149

Mistake! 157

My Choice 159

Believe It or Not	171
Shabbos for Shoshana	178
Surprise	182
Teen Extreme	189
The Promise	198
Today Is Forever	204
Within	209
Wishes at the Window	214
Reach for the Sun	222
Comfort	230
Accepting	234
Journey	240

PREFACE:

Dream On

With a flourish, I sign my name on the paper in front of me. Rikki signs afterward. Then, I read the contents on the square note aloud: "We, Rikki Marks and Malka Katzman, promise to publish a book for teens on the fun and adventure of this age, on December 15, 2009. Signed, Rikki Marks, Malka Katzman. *Bli neder.*"

I take a look at Rikki, and she smirks. I smile. She grins. I chuckle. She laughs. And we both burst into a fit of giggles.

"What a great fantasy! Come on, when we will read this in 2009 — um, what will we be by then? Mothers already, hopefully?! We will have the best laugh!" I say after we pull ourselves together.

"If we even still keep in touch then…" Rikki adds.

"Don't you dare!" I shoot Rikki a warning look. "We are keeping in touch forever and ever!"

"And ever and ever."

Good. We said it. That is most important. What could be of greater consequence for us teens than to be friends forever and ever and ever and ever?

During late night talks, when we finally finish studying and should really be sleeping already, and actually *are* sleeping already — according to our mothers — Rikki and I plan our book.

First, there are the absolutely vital details to work out: How many pages will the book have? How much will we charge for it in the bookstores? (Go tell us it's got nothing to do with us. In our fairytale version, we would write a book and become rich from it by the next day. How exactly that would happen didn't actually occur to us.) How will the cover look? (Again, in our fairytale world, we did everything for the book ourselves, although neither of us could do more than hold a pencil.)

And on to the more interesting stuff: What will be the characters' names?

We debate the names for conversations on end — and actually, we never really finish. We consider "Nechama" and "Sarah," then deliberate about "Tehilla" and even "Genendy." We argue between "Shani" and "Naava" and "Goldie" and "Esther," but alas, we cannot find common ground. In the end, Rikki goes for "Nechama" and "Shani," and I, for "Tehilla" and "Esther," respectively.

We draw up our characters' lives, while getting really confused about who is talking about whom. Sometimes Rikki starts with something like, "So Nechama went to Shani's house to help her set up the surprise birthday party," and I continue with, "And Tehilla forgot to bring the cupcakes, so Esther decided to defrost some cake and make rum balls." Then Rikki breaks in with, "But we're in *Shani's* house, right? So why is Esther — wait, Tehilla..." And I rush to correct her: "No, we are in *Esther's* house, and *Tehilla* forgot..."

At this point, Rikki usually bursts out with, "Well, actually, we're in *my* house!" and we both collapse on her living room sofa in giggles.

By the time high school rolls around, we have a semi-story planned out, except for some unresolved issues that we can't agree on. But in 2009, when we'll be a few solid years older, we'll probably be mature enough to work these things out, right? In the meantime, we can dream...

In our story, we have winter Shabbatons, fall and spring trips, and monthly vacation days where our characters do the most exotic and fun things ever heard of in high school galaxy. We have play practice for four months, before the actual play, which is held several times over another month, so that our characters only have real school for five months, minus the Yamim Tovim. We're only sorry we aren't publishing the book while we're still in high school ourselves, so our principal can get some good ideas from us!

So why don't we actually go about publishing our book then, you ask? Maybe because dreaming is more fun than doing.

Getting the book out into the real world would somehow suck the fun out of it.

My high school years are a blast, especially with such great friends as Tehilla and Esther, and Rikki, with Nechama and Shani. Actually, there is one thing Rikki and I do agree on — how our friends look. So Tehilla and Nechama are identical, and so are Esther and Shani. Tehilla/Nechama is tall and thin, with dark eyes and blond hair (we love paradoxes), and a light blue clip on her ponytail. Esther/Shani is broad but not fat, of medium height, and with straight, black pageboy-styled hair and freckles. She also has a bracelet with fourteen charms (one for every year of her life).

But as I already mentioned, the two of us can barely hold a pencil, so we can't draw our heroines. Never fear, though: our characters are more real than ever — certainly more than algebra variables.

Very surprisingly, high school comes to an end. I say "very surprisingly," because, isn't high school the center of the universe, and doesn't it go on forever? I mean, what else is there really in life?

But then one day, I am on one side of the Atlantic and Rikki is on the other, and we are chatting on the phone while trying to keep our infants relaxed. Then, strangely, there are more important things to talk about than Tehilla and Esther, or Nechama and Shani. And suddenly, I remember.

I peek at the calendar. Yup, December 15, 2009.

"Rikki, our promise!" I exclaim.

Instantly, she knows what I am talking about. "Oh my goodness! I can't believe this! Today is really December 15!"

"And the year is 2009," I add. "We never believed it would come."

We burst into good, nostalgic laughter.

"So, how are Tehilla and Esther doing?"

"And Nechama and Shani?"

"We said we'd grow up at this point, so can we please now decide on names?"

As if on cue, both our infants suddenly begin shrieking, and we have no choice but to say a quick goodbye and hang up the phone with each other.

But after little Shloimy is settled, there is suddenly nothing more important to do than continue with my old dream.

It is not Tehilla and Esther's story that my fingers itch to pen, though; it is my own story and the stories of people around me.

I sit down to write.

And I am writing every since.

❧ ❧ ❧

It began with a dream and ended in reality. I must continue to dream, because in some way, those dreams…they're all that are really mine.

On the Move

Chapter One

August

The trees are flowers in the ground. The skyscrapers look like matchboxes. Goodbye, world of mine...

"Orange juice or soda, ma'am?"

I am startled by the sudden call and turn sharply to the stewardess who is speaking to me. She looks kind; her smile makes me feel a little less alone.

I sip thoughtfully when, suddenly, I feel an abrupt jolt, and orange juice spills all over my skirt. There is turbulence.

The pilot's voice is heard over the loudspeaker. "Passengers, please fasten your seatbelts."

My heart drops with another sudden dive of the airplane. I murmur words of Tehillim, while feeling chills all over my body. I have no one's hand to squeeze. I'm traveling alone, all by myself...

But I see I'm not alone. A *Chassidishe* man sits a few seats ahead of me. I watch him as he sways back and forth, praying for all he is worth. I feel calmer. As two *frum* Jews, we're in this together. United we fly, united we pray.

Finally, our prayers are answered; the turbulence ends. My heart returns to my chest and my stomach settles down. Ah... *baruch Hashem!*

I unfasten my seatbelt and take a walk around the airplane. My eyes comb the passengers. There are men, women, children, babies... Some are sleeping, some are eating, some are talking, and some are reading. It is fascinating. I could stare at people for hours if it weren't so terribly impolite.

The woman at my right is staring and doing nothing. I've already been through a nap and a word game with myself, and she still has not seemed to move. The screen in front of me announces three and a half hours to go. We've been in the air already for four hours. Doesn't she have anything to do? I shudder. What is she thinking? Where is she headed? Does she have anything to look forward to?

Oh, well. Guess I can't count on a schmoozing partner for this trip. Another word game will have to do.

I GAZE ABOUT the bustling airport. People are snoring in their chairs. Others are checking their watches and chattering rapidly into their phones. Children are running around in circles until one falls and bawls loudly. No one looks at me.

I place a four-dollar-a-minute call on a payphone. I assure my mother that I am fine. I ate, I slept, and I will be okay. Yes, I will make sure to wait at the right gate, and to get there early. I won't miss my connecting flight. No, I will not accept anything from strangers.

I press my nose to a large window showing a glimpse of Italy. I saw Italy's boot shape from the airplane window as we approached it, and now, here I am. Am I on the heel or on the toe of the boot? It thrills me to be on foreign shores, independent and mature. I can travel the world on my own! It is mine for the taking! Oh, the possibilities that are out there…!

And yet, amid all the excitement, I'm feeling a definite thread of nervousness. Moving to a different place is like giving up a whole part of yourself. Can I do that? My body is traversing the continents today. How long will it take for my heart and mind to do the same?

I finally sit down and realize that my feet are shaking. I am so, so tired. Exhilaration is tiring. Anticipation is exhausting. I want to rest, to take a break from the wild chase of thoughts in my mind. I shut my eyes. But I don't sleep. I cannot. I don't want to miss my flight. I don't want to miss the moment.

Instead, I let my mind wander, and tears intantly spring to my eyes. I am scared to move to Israel.

I look around sheepishly, wondering who saw me cry. But nobody is looking, and I really don't even care. This is a place for tears. Airports have always been one of my favorite places. I love seeing people hug and cry, to see them being real. There is something beneath all that outside stuff, a whole inner world inside people's hearts.

And there is something inside me. An inner self I really don't know. I have brown, straight hair, green eyes, glasses. But who am I?

"Flight 35, to the gate."

I stuff my corn chips into my bulging backpack and zip it up. I take my passport and ticket in my hand, feeling like an adult, and follow the sea of humanity that is walking, walking, walking.

I stop in my tracks. That woman is familiar. I must have met her once before. I rush to catch up to her. Oh! I almost laugh out loud. I don't know her. She's just a *frum* woman, and that's the only thing familiar here. She notices me and turns her head. I smile, and she smiles back. We continue walking to our gate.

"Are you alone?" she asks suddenly.

"Yes."

"Oh! And you must be excited to be visiting Israel, aren't you?"

Tears well up in my eyes. I am not visiting Israel; I am moving to Israel. And I am so alone. Although my parents will be joining me soon, the fact is, when it will come to attending school and making friends…they won't be able to help me much. I'll be truly on my own.

I suddenly feel small. I am not an adult. I am just a kid. And I have left everything I've known for a mysterious future.

Am I excited? Am I happy?

I don't know.

✻ ✻ ✻

A CIGARETTE PUFF blows into my face. "Need help?" The blonde woman in slacks is already lugging my suitcase off the revolving pick-up stand before I can answer.

"Thank you — *todah!*"

These Israelis are helpful. A surge of emotion fills me. I am in the land of my people, whether they are wearing pants or skirts, hair coverings or gelled curls.

I am waiting for my sisters and nieces. I grip my suitcase to keep steady. I will fall if I don't. I am tired. My hair is stringy, my clothes rumpled. I just need a shower and a bed.

Scenes whiz before me. People embracing and crying. People whooping and laughing. People posing for pictures. Little people pulling away from their grandparents' embrace.

"Malka! Malka!"

Welcome signs dance around me. I fall into a sister's arms. Little nieces gape at me. Everyone is chattering at the same time. I have come home.

✻ ✻ ✻

I AWAKEN ON THE GREEN COUCH in my married brother's house and squint in the yellow sunlight. It is one o'clock in the afternoon. I have slept for sixteen hours straight! I jump up and rush to wash *negel vasser*. Enough sleeping and being tired — I can't wait to explore everything that my new life has to offer!

I sit down to the lunch my sister-in-law has prepared, listening to my niece's and nephew's happy chatter around me. The breaded chicken cutlets are soft and delicious. The potatoes and gravy fill me with a satisfaction I haven't felt in the last almost-twenty-four hours of soggy microwaved omelets, canned orange juice, and bagged pretzels.

My stomach flip-flops for just a second as the thought strikes me: *I have left America for good — practically, halachically, mentally, er — emotionally?* But I push the thought away quickly; I am too busy now to dwell on it.

A little bit later, I walk over to my sister Chaya's house. But she has no time for blasé talk. She is concerned.

"In two days you are going on the high school overnight trip. You have to be prepared." She gets down to business. "Show me what you're planning to wear."

The burnt orange tee-shirt and black slinky skirt don't impress her.

"We have to go shopping," she says.

Shopping. At nine o'clock p.m.

Welcome to Israel's night life, where stores can be hopping until ten or even eleven p.m.

The stores are full and noisy, and my head spins. I nearly yelp when Chaya shows me a navy three-piece outfit.

"I should wear *that* on a sleepover trip?"

Chaya gives me her best big-sister look. "You have to fit in. This is what the girls are wearing."

I yawn, and she has won.

I walk out with a bulging shopping bag, mourning my cool and comfy tees. But, hey, I've got to fit in.

Chapter Two

August

The mirror makes a face. I laugh. It laughs back to me. Good — I'm finally ready. I peek into my suitcase. Brushes? Check. Hair clips? Check. Outfits? Check. Shoes? Check. Slippers? Check. All that is missing is me. I zip up the suitcase and grab the handle. Bnos Yerushalayim, here I come!

Big Sister Chaya always knows best, and if she said it was worth coming to Israel alone, before my parents, to attend this two-day summer sleepover with my future classmates, I believe her. I will make friends, and I will start off twelfth grade as one of the crowd.

Chaya, bless her, accompanies me to the school. Already from afar I can see a line of buses snaking down the block. My stomach takes a lurch.

"You'll do just great, Malka!" Chaya whispers.

I smile and wave. I'll do just great.

I get onto the coach bus, surveying thirty-two new faces. As soon as I sit down, the girls surround me.

"Say a sentence in English!"

"Now a few sentences together. And fast, like all those Americans!"

I show off my English till I'm nearly blue in the face. But I don't mind. Bottom line: might that somehow earn me a friend?

It isn't long before the excitement wears off, and the girls are soon babbling in rapid, rolling Hebrew again. Cliques form in knots, and I immediately make out the who's who of the class.

I am none of them.

So the window entertains me in the meantime. Hills and lush trees speed past me. Eretz Yisrael. The land flowing with milk and honey (or chocolate spread, which is obvious by the sandwiches appearing out of knapsacks). The golden sun warms me through the windows. Ah…the light of Eretz Yisrael.

Someone is calling me. "Em…Malka?"

I spin around. Two girls are laughing.

"This-is-ponytail, no?" One of the girls points to the long, dark mane flowing down her back.

"Ye-es." I smile. Will I become the English-argument arbitrator?

The dark-haired girl (what's her *name*?) shoots the other girl an "I told you so" look. My head is still turned, but they are soon absorbed in their conversation again.

Slowly, but surely... I try to encourage myself. *Rome wasn't built in a day.*

There is a sudden tumult around me. Oh, we have arrived. Everyone is scrambling off the bus, cheering, shouting, running, laughing. Only I walk, trying to keep up.

Girls and luggage of all heights and colors zoom down a long path toward a white one-story building in the center of what looks like a massive campus. The girls place their luggage in an even line outside and then run in to the auditorium to grab a seat. Everyone knows just what to do and where to go. How, pray tell? Are there signals flashing somewhere? Do they have a secret code?

It takes me a second to realize, *Hey, silly, that's a* language. *They're following instructions. You just don't understand what the teacher is saying.* Phew, am I out of touch! I didn't even notice the teacher announcing instructions.

Welcome to the dizzying life of a newcomer.

The sudden hush is deafening. I am sitting on a chair among rows and rows of ponytailed girls, listening to a smiling woman standing on the stage.

"*Banot yekarot* (Dear girls)..."

I almost burst out laughing. Talk about gushy, effusive Israelis. Who in America would address someone "dear" like that?

Proud American that you are, I chide myself. *Don't deny that you* wish someone would lavish a little Israeli attention on *you.*

Before I know it, there is a wild applause. *Oh, no, what now?* I feel faint. The explosion of stimuli is getting to me. I'm becoming tired plowing through this thick fog of the unknown and not understood. I want to shut down and retort to anyone or anything that dares provoke my ignorance, "Me no understand. Me no understand! ME NO UNDERSTAND!"

Talking of fainting, that's not far-fetched, because I'm starving. No, I didn't munch on a chocolate sandwich on the way, nor eat anything else. You don't notice you're hungry when you're nervous, but I guess at some point it gets to you.

The girls are now all filing out of the building. Where to? I sneeze as a medley of spicy smells assaults me. Ah...to the lunchroom.

Pitas, hummus, soy burgers. Eggplant dip and spicy tomato salad. Oh — chicken nuggets! Rippled French fries! Ketchup!

I send up a silent thanks to Hashem. *Thank You for the normal food, so I don't have to gag on cumin and hot paprika.*

My face feels hot as I try to elegantly make a plate for myself of some nuggets and fries. I feel like everyone is looking at me, taunting, "New girl, new girl, you are the new girl."

There are leaflets on the table. Oh, a schedule. I check the program for one thirty. *Hartza'ah.*

"Um..." I point to the word, addressing the girl near me with questioning eyes.

"*Hartza'ah*," she says loudly. "*Mishehu midebar, hartza'ah.*"

Midebar — talking. Who? What? When?

My friend for the moment is already chattering with someone else again. I guess I'll have to find out the answers to my questions on my own.

We are in the lecture hall, and someone is talking, all right. And talking. And talking. And I am inspired — by the desperate need to understand the language of my land.

A band strikes up a song. "*V'taher libeinu.*" Oh, goody — this I can understand. I crane my neck to watch the pianist. Wow, she can't be more than a ninth or tenth grader. And hey, that's another high school girl, playing the violin. She looks like a real natural. And that flutist just completes this harmonious scene. These Israelis sure are talented. I've heard that almost every Israeli girl takes some kind of extracurricular class in the afternoons (which, on average, start at two o'clock). Compare that with us biology-and-chemistry-book-porers in the good ol' U.S. of A. It's just a different science, what can I tell you?

The rest of the girls are not only singing. They are standing, clapping, holding hands, waving arms. Orchestrating motions in perfect synchronization. Effusive, energetic...Israelis. Thanks for the entertainment.

The slow, poignant song comes to an end, and a lively song begins to play. The girls race to the large empty area in the hall and grab each other's hands. I find myself swept into a raucous dance whose steps I can't follow. Some girls smile at me; others wink, as if we're the best of friends sharing a secret. Everyone seems perfectly confident that I am adjusting beautifully. Maybe they each think someone else is befriending me, and so they can be free to have a good time.

Good for them.

Everyone is red-faced by the time the music stops. The cold drinks are refreshing. I am debating which girl to try for a conversation, when someone taps my shoulder. It is a teacher, smiling broadly.

"You're Malka, right? Nice to meet you!" Her English is actually understandable. I smile and nod. "Have a good time!" she says, giving me a friendly pat on the arm before she turns away.

The gesture warms me, like a cup of hot tea on a cold winter day.

The girls are soon seated in a large, darkened auditorium. "*Seret*," one girl explains to me. A film. It looks intriguing, and I try to follow. A woman kidnapping a girl, police interrogating her…blurrrr.

…I rub my eyes and yawn. What? Why is everyone filing out of the auditorium? Is the film over? Did I…did I actually sleep through the whole thing? I want to cry, feeling so stupid to have done that. Oh, how I wish I could just wake up and find myself back home, telling my friends about the strangest dream I ever had…

I bolt to the door and try to catch up with "my" class. I am embarrassed and avoid meeting anyone's eyes.

I am soon walking upstairs with my luggage to find myself a room for the night. I come when the others have already secured beds for themselves. One girl — I think I heard someone call her Gila — kindly shows me that Room Three has an empty bed.

There are three girls already in Room Three. When they see me enter, they call out a cheerful, "Hi!" in unison.

I smile and realize that my mouth is quivering.

"Welcome," one of the girls, a redhead, adds. She looks nice.

She points to a closet. I open my luggage, pull out a semi-creased outfit, and hang it up. I keep busy arranging my things in a single drawer, and then I have nothing more to do.

I sit down on my bed, across from my chattering roommates, and suck in a hopeful breath.

"*Mah hashem shelach* (What is your name)?"

Tehilla. Gila. Chedva. Strains of "*Gila…ditza v'chedvah*" play in my mind. They're the happy trio, aren't they? Glad to be here.

Or am I?

We've exchanged names, but now they're off to another planet. They are busy with who came and who's sleeping in whose room and which teacher will chaperon on the trip. Who came? And where are the rooms? And *which* trip?

I just want to go to sleep.

I sit like a deaf-mute, staring ahead but not really seeing. It's easy to say, "Hi, what's your name?" It's not so easy to stick it out for a whole conversation. Who has patience for polite chitchat when you can rattle a-mile-a-minute about the real, good stuff?

A film forms over my eyeballs, and I — no, I will *not* cry. I cannot cry here. I *must* cry, but I *must not*. I want to cry, but oh, how I don't want to!

I jump to my feet. The bathroom is just a few steps away. If only I can —

"Oh, are you going already?" Tehilla says to me in slow Hebrew.

I blink. My eyes are safely dry.

I smile. "Um…no, I'm not."

The rock in my throat slides down. Maybe I can give it another chance.

Chapter Three

September

The briefcase feels weird in my hands. I haven't carried one since eighth grade. In my high school in New York, we took notes and put all our stuff in big three-ring binders, which we carried in our arms. I sling the briefcase over my shoulder. It's heavy. It is filled with a stack of notebooks (remember those?) painstakingly labeled with the names of the fifteen or so subjects in the twelfth-grade curriculum — *Ge'ographiah, Historiah, Yahadut, Matimatika, Anglit,* you name it.

A neighbor starting ninth grade this year kindly offers to walk with me to school. It is only 8:10 a.m. (oh, to return to those days when I could open my first eye at that time, with school not starting until 9:00 a.m!), but the streets are crowded with throngs of excited girls and boys. The sun is bright, and the air is fresh. It is the first day of school.

A lively *"Bruchim Haba'im"* song plays in the school building when we arrive. My neighbor smiles to me and hesitantly waves goodbye. I smile and wish her *hatzlachah*. Hers is also a momentous first day.

I am lost in a sea of blue. Girls, girls, and more girls in crisp uniforms swarm around me — short girls, tall girls, quiet girls, loud girls, smiling girls, anxious girls. Which will be my friend?

I think back to the overnight trip and remember Tehilla. She looked kind, smart, and really my type. Problem is, she didn't really make much of an effort to befriend me, except for a shy "welcome," in the beginning. But maybe, just maybe, today will be different.

A crackle interrupts the music, and a loud voice is heard over the loudspeaker: "*Bruchot habaot, na l'hikanes lakitot* (Welcome; please enter your classrooms)."

I turn right and left, north and south. Where is my classroom? The lobby empties quickly. I frantically check the doors of the classrooms encircling the lobby: 11-1, 11-2, 11-5 (5?! How many *classes* are there per grade?). No class 12 in sight.

The hallways are completely empty by now. My heartbeat races. *Help!* I climb up a flight of stairs and check the line of classroom doors. 12-1! Finally! I push open the door.

Immediately, thirty or so pairs of eyes are on me. The teacher steps down from the small podium at the front of the class and looks me up and down. "Em — I don't think you are in this class," she says in a Hebrew that I can thankfully understand. I stand frozen. What should I do now?

"*Rega* (one minute)," she calls out to the class and walks out of the room, beckoning me after her. She leads me to the office, and after a quick exchange with the secretary, tells me in English, "Class 12-4" and points down the hallway.

My feet are wobbling by the time I enter class 12-4. The teacher is in the middle of talking, and again, about thirty pairs of eyes, albeit somewhat familiar ones, stare up at me. The teacher stops mid-sentence and looks at me, smiling broadly.

"Malka! We wait for you!"

I try to smile in return, but I don't know if I am doing a good job. My eyes sweep the classroom. Everyone is seated in partners at double desks. One girl is sitting on her own at the far right of the classroom, and the teacher points to the empty seat near her, urging me to take a seat there. I sit down on the edge of the plastic chair, still clutching my briefcase. The teacher continues with what she was saying before I came in, and the girls' attention shifts back to her. Finally, the show is over.

I listen to the teacher intently, picking up some familiar words and some coherent sentence fragments. I'm so glad I (usually) listened in *Ivrit* class at school back in New York. My teacher there was intent on getting us to speak Hebrew. I remember how we'd roll our eyes when she made us repeat her heavily-accented Hebrew sentences. If only I could go back and repeat those sentences again now. Let my American friends laugh as I break my teeth, but oh, just not my Israeli peers here!

Luckily for me, the second class is the history of World War I, which I have already learned. I am going to be a student like all the others and take notes.

"*Hamilchamah hit'chilah b'elef tesha me'ot v'arba esrei,*" the teacher begins, and I write, "The war began in 1914." So far, so good. She lists the countries on the Allies' side, and I write in English, "England, France, Italy."

The ring of the bell coincides with a throbbing in my head. I am dizzy and nauseous. Forty-five minutes of painstaking translating half-comprehensible Hebrew is enough for me to call it a day.

But before I can get up to stretch, I see the history teacher gesturing to me. "Come here, please, Malka," she says in English. Recess banter swirls around me as I make my way to the teacher's desk at the front of the room.

"Welcome, Malka. I am glad we are joined by such a conscientious student. I noticed you were taking notes. Mind if I take a look at your notebook?"

Her flawless English surprises and warms me. I retrieve my history notebook from my desk and hand it to her. She opens it and smiles. "Wow — this is...*professional!* You should be earning double the pay than the rest of the class!" She winks. "Your translation is really great."

She pauses thoughtfully. "I lived in England for a chunk of my elementary school years, so I have a little experience with learning in a different language. I found that the best way to really get into the language was to take notes in English, and not in my native Hebrew. And it worked." She laughs. "It was sometimes funny. I remember once writing a title of a new topic in a *Hilchos Shabbos* class: 'The Big Day Shabbos' — when it really was '*Bigdei Shabbos* (Shabbos clothing)!' I was trying so hard that I interpreted everything as English, but you see, I turned out fine in the end."

The teacher puts a hand on my shoulder, and I instinctively step back. "Think about it, Malka. I'm sure you'll do well."

I return to my classmates. Everyone is eating, talking, and laughing. "*Aruchat eser* (ten o'clock meal)," they called it. I'd already eaten breakfast in the morning at home — toast, eggs, cheese. Here, breakfast was…you guessed it, chocolate sandwiches.

I look around, hoping to see Tehilla. I finally spot her, deeply involved in a conversation with two other girls. I imagine her coming to me and starting a conversation, maybe even inviting me to her house to do homework. But no such luck. The bell for the next class is ringing.

My desk partner, whose name is Lalli (with perpetually flushed cheeks that actually remind me of two red lollipops), tells me, "*Navi*.. We now learn *Navi*."

I smile. It is nice of her to update me.

During *Navi* class, I try to write in Hebrew, peeking at Lalli's perfect, tiny scrawls when I miss something. I watch her underline titles with a ruler and carefully white out the tiniest speck of a mistake. My scribbles cannot compete, but by the end of the class, I am still proud. I took notes in Hebrew. I could do it. I am really getting somewhere!

A jingle plays on the loudspeaker, and my classmates grab their briefcases and race out the door. Oh — we've been dismissed.

I just cannot wait to get home.

But how? I have no clue which direction to even take! I look around the school lobby, but among the hundreds of girls, I know it will be a miracle to find my neighbor. I have to be brave.

I walk out of the school building and stop a girl. "Rechov Gershom...*eizeh kivun* (which direction)?"

She thinks for a moment, then says in Hebrew, "Come with me. I'm going in that direction."

She walks with her friends, and I trail after them. I feel friendless and alone in a world where everyone knows everyone (or so it seems), but at least I'm on my way HOME!

The smell of chicken and steamed string beans greets me when I walk through the door.

"In honor of your first day of school," my mother says, "we'll eat dinner at noon, Israeli style."

I am grateful for that, as the warm food sliding down my throat comforts me.

"So?" my mother asks, looking at me.

My forkful of chicken stops in midair. I must show some hope, even if I feel no such thing.

"It's...hard to tell. There are...some nice girls. I'm sure I'll make friends soon."

Yeah, right. My friends are an ocean away. Forget about it.

"And how was class?"

I shrug. "All right, I guess. I'm gonna get used to it one day."

Will I?

My mother wants to hear more, but I cannot try being cheery anymore. All I want to do is close my eyes and go to sleep... Yes, that's what I'll do. The Israeli folk are big advocates of taking a daytime nap; they call it *menuchat tzaharayim* — an afternoon rest. *Menuchah* is just what I need. I escape to my room and pull the covers over my head.

Sleep was never so sweet.

Chapter Four

October

There's more to life than school. Yamim Tovim roll around, and a familiar joy creeps into my heart. It's family time, off-from-school time — and that's all over the world. Some things *do* stay the same.

Well, not exactly the same, because here the school really carves out a lot more vacation time for us high school girls, so we can help at home. Now that's a welcome change! I'm off to my sisters, peeling, sifting, mixing, and tasting. With a three-day Rosh Hashanah this year, we've got loads to prepare.

That's how I discover my love for the kitchen. And the best part is that there, it doesn't matter which language you speak. So I tie my apron strings and learn the kitchen's secrets, from chicken soup to chocolate truffles.

But that still can't compare to the joy in the Israeli Rosh Hashanah experience. Eretz Yisrael is a spiritual place, and that's a fact. It's in the air, in the people, in the places you go. Erev Rosh Hashanah is Erev Rosh Hashanah for everyone (or almost everyone) in Israel. Everyone is preparing for the New Year, at least to some degree.

And that's something for me to think about. How am *I* preparing for the New Year? This is a whole different type of New Year for me, and it better be some Rosh Hashanah. This year in shul, I find that *davening* takes on a whole new dimension. The year ahead is truly so unknown, a real big question mark.

Sometimes I have to look around, pinch myself, look around again, and only then do I begin to truly realize that this is real. My life has changed, probably permanently. I think of myself *there*, in my New York neighborhood, in my beloved high school uniform, trotting to school with a bulging loose-leaf under my arm. Then I think of myself *here*, under the sunny Israeli skies, juggling an overloaded briefcase, on my way to my new Israeli school… Are both pictures of myself really me?

Change makes me realize that there is something very deep and intrinsic inside of me that remains the same, no matter where I am or what I'm wearing or what I'm carrying. If I'm only who I am because of my uniform or loose-leaf, it may really be hard to believe that I am still me now that those aspects have changed.

But my uniform is *not* me: I am something much greater, more existential than that. "Soul" is a deep word, but it's really the truth of who I am, and finding it means finding me.

Here in Eretz Yisrael, when it's time for *tekiyas shofar*, the shofar blows in shuls all over the country. Everyone is *davening*, everyone is running to hear the shofar, everyone is hoping for a good year. It's nice to be part of something bigger, to be part of hopes and dreams larger than yourself.

During the Aseres Yemei Teshuvah, we have all of three days of school. The rest of the days are spent at home; they are days to connect with family and with yourself.

❋❋❋

WHEN SUKKOS WINKS with glittering colors, the momentum of things really picks up. I visit Yerushalayim one day, and the colorful, musical preparations are exhilarating. It is Sukkos wherever you turn: planks of wood, *s'chach*, sukkah decorations, "*V'samachta B'chagecha*" songs. It's like everyone here is one big family, all preparing for Yom Tov together. Yes, we *are* really one family, no matter how different our *minhagim* may be from each other's. The inside is all the same.

Now what's a visit to Yerushalayim without stopping at the Kosel? The Kosel is an old friend by now. It embraces me morning, noon, or night. Night is falling now, and a chill creeps into the air. I don't feel cold, though. The Kosel is warm and loving and inviting. I whisper the words of Maariv, one hand on the cold stones. Behind this wall…what could be there, what *should* be there... I sigh. Our enemies are in that place instead, at the moment ululating prayers over the microphone.

Sudden drops sprinkle my siddur. I look up to the velvet sky, and another drip wets my cheek like a teardrop. The drizzle comes as a surprise — it doesn't usually rain here in the autumn — but I enjoy the feel of the raindrops licking my neck.

I finish *davening*, and start a slow backward trek, never taking my eyes off the Wall. How many people have walked this same reluctant walk, under the same starry sky, hoping and dreaming the same dreams?

But when Sukkos actually comes and I am sitting in my family's hot sukkah, I find myself wishing that I was shivering in our sukkah back in New York instead. What is it about memories that make the past seem so tempting, even when it was really cold and rainy and dreary back then? I guess I don't really miss shivering; I miss being in my old place, being my old self.

Can I always be my old self? Yes and no. Some parts of me will always remain the same — but I also changed, and I cannot turn back the clock.

And, the truth is, I really shouldn't want to.

✼ ✼ ✼

SIMCHAS TORAH BRINGS ME some comfort. My family rents an apartment in Yerushalayim, and we experience Yom Tov in the electrifying atmosphere there. Somehow, in Yerushalayim one always feels at home, even more so than in one's actual home. No, it's not the bed with the nearly paper-thin mattress that makes me feel this way. It is the air around me that is homey; the special, intrinsic feeling that this is Yerushalayim, the home of Hashem. And as a bonus, the sukkah *is* chilly there. We don't have to eat the *seudos* in the sukkah, but we do huddle there in our sweaters, drinking tea and tapping our feet to the song embracing us from all directions.

The Torah is in the streets here. We stop at a yard where a group of Sephardi men and boys dance around and around in circles. Past the circles is a tiny trailer that must be their shul. I guess they can't dance there. So they break free and dance up a storm on the streets. It looks like their enthusiasm would've taken them there anyway.

There is so much to see. We stop at Satmar, and at Belz, and at some unfamiliar shuls. Some are big, and some are small. Some don't have a women's section, but it ends up forming on the street, along the side of the shul. Everything seems to vibrate — the buildings, the streets, my heart. The singing engulfs me like a huge sea, and I ride on the waves, on the high notes and low notes, and have the time of my life.

This must be a tiny inkling of the joy that will be in the Beis Hamikdash in this very magical city, when Mashiach comes. May it be soon and in our times!

Chapter Five

December

I've started a new schedule, waking up at midnight each night. I mean, I wake up every day in the morning, at 7:15 a.m., but midnight is when I *really* perk up. My friends in the good ol' U.S. of A. are just about to come home from school then, and we can start schmoozing. The house is quiet, and I get settled, cross-legged, on my bed, the door of my room shut. A small nightlight shines on the night table. I talk quietly, so no one will hear me and wake up.

A new day is starting for me.

Rikki is first today. I haven't spoken to her in aaaages — I mean, since two nights ago. How did the science test go? What happened with her brother's sprained ankle? When is the Tu B'Shevat *chagigah* scheduled for? I've been in the dark for too long.

The other side of the line is noisy. Cutlery clatters and kids bicker. "Mommy, can I take another burger?" Rikki's voice rattles into the phone. She is chewing with real gusto, making me hungry. "It's burgers tonight, with fresh baguettes and lettuce. Yum!"

"Oooh…can I join?"

"Come on in!"

"I wish. Remember the good old days? Once a week at my house, once a week at yours."

"That was fun."

"Rikki — will that really never happen again?"

"Maybe it could. Where'd you say you were up to? Two hundred dollars? Keep on saving, and you'll be flying before you know it!"

"By the rate I'm going, it ain't happening so fast." I scowl. I have only one hundred dollars in savings, after I have already shelled out another hundred on the international line set up especially for me. My dream visit seems like, well, a dream.

"Oh, Rikki, you didn't tell me who won Color War!"

"I didn't tell you? Oh — that's because we lost."

"Aw. How's that, if your team scored forty more points on the theme song?"

"We got forty more points? I didn't know! How did *you* know?"

We laugh. "Let's just say I overheard it in the office. But seriously, Chani told me. You can go ahead and test me, Rik. I know more than you would believe."

"Okay, so then tell me, which teacher was absent today?"

"You'll have to fill me in this time."

Mrs. Gustman is away for a *simchah* for a week. The substitute is a fascinating teacher. And Fraidy is sick at home with the flu for a week already. Mindy got a short haircut. There will be a *tzedakah*-a-thon in school tomorrow. The science test was a breeze.

At this last tidbit, I grumble, "Well, good for you, but science here is just *impossible*. I'm hearing ten new words per minute, and I just lose everything. Maybe you wanna help me study for *my* science test?"

"If only I could, Malka, really. I feel so bad for you."

"Me, too. Studying used to be so much fun. Remember when we studied once for a Chumash test together until three in the morning?"

"Sure do. You know, I miss your room. There was nothing like lying down on that plush carpet and studying —"

"Or falling asleep. Remember you fell asleep right on the floor until the morning? I tried to wake you up to study more, but you wouldn't budge."

"Hmmmph — how would I forget? It became the joke of the class."

"You know, Rikki, you said you miss my room? You better believe I do, too." I try not to cry. "Sometimes I wish we could've somehow brought my yummy green carpet here —"

"How about just bringing *you* back?"

Now I am crying, and I don't try to stop.

Rikki doesn't talk.

It feels good to cry; I could go on for hours.

"I wish I could help you somehow," Rikki finally says.

We hang up on a sad note. I feel tears coming from deep inside me, like a fountain. I cry and cry and cry. It's so hard. It's so hard. I fall asleep with tears drying on my face.

* * *

THE SUNLIGHT BLINDS ME. It can't be morning already. I squint at the digits on the alarm clock. Eight o'clock.

Groan. My back feels like a wooden board. I've been up till three, and I'm tired. I don't care if it's eight o'clock. For me it's one in the morning, American time.

The next thing I know, it is one thirty p.m.

My mother's note is on the counter, near a covered plate of hard-boiled eggs and salad. My mother has left for some errands and didn't want to wake me. She knew I must have been tired from a week of Chanukah parties (ha, ha).

Well, I'm not leaving for no school. School will be over in a half hour.

I enjoy my breakfast with the school newsletter that Rikki mailed me. Updates, *mazel tovs*, short stories, tidbits. Good old school.

I grab a sheet from a notebook. I want to write my own entry for the next school newsletter.

Dear good old friends...

I am crying again.

I finish a short letter and fax it immediately to the submission fax line. I can be part of things in my own way.

At three, I dial Perel for a quick good morning call. She promises she will send regards to the class.

I hang up, and the phone rings instantly. Lalli, my desk partner at school, is on the line.

"We missed you today."

I blush. Did she say someone missed me? "Oh, uh, yeah, I couldn't come today."

"You're not feeling well?"

"Uh, yeah, sort of." Is being tired counted as not feeling well?

"Oh. Today, Hamorah (Teacher) Rosenfeld taught about the American government and the Constitution, and she told us that she'd wanted to ask you if you ever visited Washington, and if you did, if you could tell us a little about it."

I am too surprised to speak.

"So will you come tomorrow and do that?"

"Of-of course."

❋ ❋ ❋

"Go ahead, Malka." Mrs. Rosenfeld is nodding. "You can get up on the podium and start. We're all ears!"

I try to steady my wobbling legs. Everyone is looking at me, expectant. I take a long breath and start. I'm going for it, for better or for worse. "To celebrate the start of high school, we were treated to a trip to Washington." I mentally pat myself on the back for my fluent Hebrew. I even said "Voshington" right.

"We left bright and early in the morning and traveled for hours. We brought lots of nosh — American nosh — and kept ourselves busy the whole ride. It was probably the best part of the trip."

I spot some smiles. Good. I smile, too, and take a deep breath.

"Well, I really have to talk about history-related stuff —"

"No, go on! Tell us about your *Amerika'i* class!"

I glance at Mrs. Rosenfeld. She nods. "You can entertain them for another little bit before the history stuff."

I continue talking…and talking — and the class just listens and listens. This is fun. I am being me. I am not the new girl, trying to fit into a new identity. I am me, talking and sharing my own experiences and thoughts.

And my classmates are listening, accepting and riveted to everything I say, mistakes included!

"It was an interesting trip," I end off by saying, "but as always, the best part is the fun of being together with friends." I bite my lip. Did I really say that? I blush as I walk back to my seat.

The teacher is going on and on about how great that was, but I can hardly hear her. I am shaking all over. I did it, and it really *was* great! I sneak a glance at the clock. I spoke for, what, is that a *half hour*? That's almost a full lesson. I did it. I did it. I did it!

At recess, girls crowd around me. They want to hear more. I talk, sip some water, and talk more. Talking about Washington turns into talking about my old school, the yearly play, and Shabbaton. Everyone is oohing and aahing and urging me to say more.

I feel like I am there, back in my old school. The classroom with double desks melts into a classroom of single desks. I look at the podium in the front of the classroom and see the regular brown teacher's desk in my old school. The closet at the front of the classroom becomes a row of cubbies, and the girls are wearing striped white and blue shirts instead of light blue ones.

But then recess is over, and I have to stop sharing. I am back in a classroom of double desks, a whiteboard, and classmates with light blue shirts.

The day passes in a daze. I have traversed continents in a few hours, and these sudden changes are unsettling. Where am I? Where do I want to be?

I have yet to answer these questions.

But I walk home with friends, and we enjoy a friendly chat. They are not old friends, they are not best friends, but they are friends.

One thing is certain. I'm glad I came to school today.

Chapter Six

January

I don't read the Israeli newspaper headlines. To read Hebrew for the sake of pure interest is too definitive an integration in Israeli society. I'm not ready for that. For now, reading Hebrew is a matter of utmost necessity only.

But now I know the headlines even without reading them. I can hear them. They scream from the sky, as airplanes rip through the heavens and buzz in our ears.

War is in the air.

I used to think war was bloody battles and wounded soldiers. It was shivering and disheveled grandmothers, mothers, and children hiding in bunkers with frightful, bloodshot eyes, awaiting the men's return from their attempts to procure food. War was growling stomachs and bony arms. It was howls, shrieks, and barks.

It was trauma. It was fear. It was hate. And it was death.

But in the here and now, I am Malka and I go to school every day. I brush my neat brown, layered hair and put on a fresh, starched uniform. My mother packs my bag with two cheese-and-vegetable sandwiches that she insists I finish, an apple, and pretzels. I enter the school building to the sound of music in the hallways and a welcome blast of air conditioning.

And my country is at war.

War and life. In this country, the two can go together.

Rockets are hitting the South now, thick and fast. But miracles bombard us even faster. Seven missiles fall in the morning…all in open areas, causing no damage. Twelve missiles rain down at lunchtime in Be'er Sheva, Ashkelon, and Ashdod…and *baruch Hashem*, everyone is safe. *Thirty* missiles falling from dusk until midnight all miss their mark. A rocket hits a building roof and doesn't explode. Three rockets in a row drown in the sea.

Hashem is here, on the battleground, fighting for us.

The people in the South are coming to us, we hear. Their children don't want to hear the sirens anymore. They are bored and disoriented, without school, parks, or outdoor play for structure or recreation.

Jews around the country invite their Southern brothers into their homes and schools. Free meals are available at the local *beis hatavshil*. Afternoon carnivals are set up by eager teens. With everyone's contributions, North and Central Israel really become the Southerners' home away from home.

We welcome a family of six into our home. As they walk in shyly through the door, I don't see any sign of those huddled, fearful children with tattered clothes. These people wheel in a set of matching suitcases and hand us a cellophane-wrapped arrangement of fruit and chocolates.

They settle down in the two bedrooms we prepared and then promptly leave, kids in tow, "for supper, and we won't be back until ten, and our kids will go to school tomorrow. And please don't prepare linen. We've brought our own." I feel bad. They are afraid to intrude.

They leave before we can even protest, and I'm sorry we didn't. I want to know what their life is like, to feel the doubt and fear with them.

What is life like, under the threat of rockets falling from the sky? How do you go about your day when you may have to take cover any minute?

"It's not as scary as you think," Shira, our thirteen-year-old guest, tells me over cookies and cocoa at ten thirty at night. "There is a siren, and you run to the nearest shelter. You hear a boom, sometimes two, or even three, and then it's over."

"Tell me more."

"Well, I'll tell you about our day yesterday:"

Someone's crying. Crying? No, no, it's the siren! I sit up, swing my feet over to the side of the bed — and straight into my negel vasser.

I consider the towel for a millisecond, but I don't reach out for it. I plunk my dripping feet onto the freezing stone floor and run. Chaya and Shmulik are already over Abba and Ima's shoulders; I race to Sarah's bed and yank her out, schlepping her across the floor after me as she whines. Finally, we are all safe, behind the closed, metal door of our sealed room.

Ahhh. Safety.

My body aches with exhaustion. Why so early?! The nerve of our Arab neighbors!

A boom explodes into my thoughts, and everything quivers. Another boom. No... I close my eyes, as if that will protect me. Finally, the air is clear. Our apartment building echoes with voices, like it is the peak of the eight o'clock rush. But it is only five forty a.m. And today there will be no eight o'clock rush; we are all home to stay for who-knows-how-much-longer.

Abba thanks Abdul and Achmad for waking him so early; at least he'll make the early minyan *today. But I don't even smile at the joke. I am angry. It's one thing when we're disturbed all day; we can't sleep peacefully, either?*

Oh, no...Shmulik is already on to trouble. I moan. Another day of in-house (sometimes in-room) "Terrible–Two" antics has started, bright and early.

"One rocket fell in an open area just one hundred meters away from here," our informed neighbor, a Hatzolah man with a constantly blaring walkie-talkie, announces. "The other one hit the roof of a building" — there is terror in everyone's eyes — "but all the people on the top floor thankfully evacuated their apartments

and were in the building bomb shelter."

The mini crowd in the building stairwell disperses quickly. Everyone is hoping to catch another little bit of sleep. Aaaarrgh...not Shmulik. He is already tugging at Ima's skirt, begging for "la-la." That's a good idea. Let us hear happy music, for a change, instead of that warning howl that never stops ringing in our ears.

I want to make hot, sweet chocolate pudding for breakfast. Ima is delighted; that will keep the kids busy for a while. She disappears into the laundry room, and I seat Shmulik and Chaya at the table to watch me make their treat.

I take out the milk and put it on the counter. Ooooh...ooooh... siren! I grab Shmulik from his high chair — after he had finally settled down — and urge Chaya to run. Sarah skips into the sealed room with her jump rope. Ima emerges from the laundry room, a pile of skirts and robes slung over her arm. Our eyes meet. We can forget our plans for today. We wait, and sigh, and tremble. And, when the all-clear signal is heard, we wordlessly return to our activities.

I read the recipe: 10 tablespoons sugar, 6 tablespoons cornstarch, 4 tablespoons cocoa, 1 quart milk. I mix the dry ingredients with a bit of milk in the pot until a smooth paste forms. Then I turn on the flame and begin pouring the bag of milk into the pot.

Just then... "Ambulance!" Shmulik screams. The siren alarms me, and the milk container drops from my hands, starting a slow stream of white across the floor. Almost slipping on the milk, I scoop up Shmulik, and we cluster in the sealed room again.

Boom, boom, boom. We don't ask anymore where the rockets fell.

They are falling everywhere, everywhere, but, oh, Hashem, just not on us, please!

We are back in the kitchen, with a smoldering pot and a burnt smell. I shut the flame, throw the crusty pot into the sink, and sit at the table with Chaya and Shmulik. I can't give them chocolate pudding, but I can give them myself and, maybe, the security that they crave.

"That's why we had to leave."

"And you know what — we're glad you came!" I tell her. "Whaddaya say, Shira, should we make chocolate pudding now?"

Shira laughs, and we get to work. The pudding bubbles and thickens as Shira stirs.

"You know what the thing is about war?" she says suddenly. "It's being unstable. You don't know what the next minute will bring. You sit on a chair with one foot ready to run. You sleep half-awake. Nothing is in your control."

"Well, isn't that like life?" I muse. "You really never know what the next minute will bring."

"But…you *think* you know."

"Right. We like being in control."

"But you know what? Who said it's good to always try to be in control? Compare me with Shmulik. He had a great time running in and out of the sealed room with the sirens. He thought it was a game. He relies on my mother for his safety and comfort. He trusts that he is being taken care of. I, on the other hand, was worried sick."

"So there's something better than being in control."

"Yes, there is. Trust."

❋ ❋ ❋

Baruch Hashem, the war soon ends. Shira and her family leave our home faster than I'd like, but hey, that must be a good thing. And life goes on, to my surprise. It makes me realize that yes, war always was, is, and will be a part of life in this land, until Mashiach comes.

Like it or not, I am living in a land whose safety is constantly at risk. I scrutinize every taxi driver, and check for suspicious packages when I ride a bus. I clench my fists when we travel through Arab-populated areas and wonder if the boys running around outside are about to pitch a rock right at my window.

But at the same time, life isn't tense in Israel. I wonder if it's because facing our mortality numbs us, or perhaps because it heightens our *bitachon*. Maybe it depends on the person — some go into denial, while others grow from the precariousness of our existence.

I hope never to shut my eyes and ears to what's going on around me, but rather to keep them wide open — and thus be capable of appreciating life so much more.

Chapter Seven

February

Dreams do come true!

It is *aruchat eser* (the ten o'clock meal) in school, and I am eating my sandwich. Yudit, a classmate, asks me to join her on a stroll around the school yard. I stifle a laugh. Like, huh? Me and Yudit? Friends? What will we *talk* about? But I don't say anything of the sort. Instead, I say, "Sure! I'll just finish *bentching* and I'll come with you."

We're strolling near the school entrance. Oh, no, we really don't have what to talk about...but, but...what's going on? Am I seeing things? I feel dizzy. Rikki. Rikki! That's Rikki there!

Could it be?

Is that really Rikki?

Rikki?

RIKKI?!

I break out in a run.

"Rikki!"

"Malka!"

We hug, and laugh, and cry.

"Rikki…are you really here?"

"I think I am!"

I scan her up and down. Yup, that is Rikki. From her shoes all the way up to her headband. Rikki is really here!!

I notice some curious spectators, and I nudge Rikki to follow me to an empty, quiet spot. We plop down on the grass, squinting in the bright sun.

"What a surprise! What a SURPRISE! Rikki, this is just…unbelievable!"

Rikki smiles. "I couldn't wait to see your reaction!"

"Now tell me every single detail. What? When? How?"

"Well, it started like this. You know we have my nephew's bar mitzvah, here in Yerushalayim, this Thursday. My parents had booked tickets just for themselves, but a few weeks ago I decided I had to come, too…to cheer you up a little, and also to see my sister and her family. It was really hard to convince my parents, but finally, finally, I won! So…here I am!"

"Rikki, you're just the best!"

We sit quietly, smiling, enjoying our happy thoughts. A shrill bell interrupts us, and we watch a sea of blue-uniformed girls streaming into the school building. Classes are going on as usual, but for me the world has stopped. I am not in Israel, not in America...I'm in no-man's land. I am in dreamland.

Time flies as Rikki and I talk and reminisce, and I feel like we could go on forever. Before we know it, the bell rings again for a short break.

"C'mon, Malka, you have to show me your class," Rikki begs.

I lead her up the staircase to my classroom, in a trance. Rikki meeting my Israeli classmates? Talk about uncanny. A juxtaposition of two worlds.

Past, present, and future...meshed into one. My life jumbled into one mix.

We walk into the noisy classroom, and it turns quiet in a second.

"H-hi, everyone...this is my friend, Rikki," I say.

Rikki, dressed in true American fashion, immediately takes the limelight. *Sneak preview!* I imagine announcing. *Introducing the latest styles soon to reach Israeli shores!*

Suddenly, I feel connected to my Israeli counterparts. Israel may be behind in fashion, but it is always ahead of the game in *ruchniyus*. I'm proud to be a part of that.

My classmates crowd around us, and I translate their curious babble to Rikki, and her broken Hebrew to them. I am both amused and embarrassed, realizing that I had sounded like Rikki just a few months ago.

My classmates ask Rikki about school in New York, the weather there, the plane ride. Rikki's news is fresh, her accent immaculate.

She's fresh off American shores, its air still on her skin. I, on the other hand, am already an oldie — a once-American.

Rikki, like a good American tourist, has a camera handy, and we pose for a picture with my class. We all scream, "Cheese!" and giggle at the flashing camera.

My smile is as wide as the room. More than capturing the moment in a photo, I want to capture the moment in my heart.

✻ ✻ ✻

Rikki sleeps at my house at night. We schmooze, nosh, and party away like there is no tomorrow. On Tuesday we take a trip to the Kosel together, on Wednesday we coast along the Tel Aviv shores in a ferry, and on Thursday we enjoy her nephew's beautiful bar mitzvah. But the best is yet to come: Rikki invites me to spend Shabbos with her at her sister's house!

As Shabbos approaches, I have mixed feelings: I can't wait for Shabbos, but I also don't want it to start. If it starts, it means that it will end.

I need, I want to buy Rikki a gift. I could never express enough gratitude for her devotion, but a gift is the least I can do. I peruse a gift shop, finally choosing a classy watch. A watch is time, but friendship is timeless. At home I write her a little poem, just a sampling of my roaring thoughts and feelings:

A friend is life;
A friend is air to breathe;
A friend is survival;
A friend should never leave.

A friend is your breakfast,
Lunch and supper, too;
A friend is your clock,
Morning, night, and noon.

But that's not all. More words spill into my mind, flowing out of my pen. I take another sheet and write, just for myself:

But without a friend...
How can I smile?
How can I be bright?
How can I see
When I am groping through the night?

The page is suddenly wet, and I let myself cry, and cry, and cry.

The Friday night meal, full of fun and camaraderie, has just ended. Oh, how I enjoyed it! I am my old self again. I am singing inside, and I want to be my old self forever. Something tells me I can, because I am who I am, with or without the people around me. But I am not yet convinced.

Rikki and I change into our nightgowns and settle in our specially-prepared bedroom. It is dark and late — the perfect time for a heart-to-heart talk.

But we sit quietly, thinking, communicating through the language of friendship and connection.

I finally break the silence. "Rikki, how will I manage when you're gone?" I try to swallow, but a lump in my throat gets in the way.

"It must be…so hard."

"You bet. You know what it's like coming to school every day without having one decent friend?"

Rikki bites her lip.

"Rikki, stay." I know it's ridiculous, but I savor the word "stay" as it echoes in my mind.

"Well, there's fantasy and there's reality."

"I go for fantasy."

So we fantasize. We imagine that I am back in my old school. We are studying for a chemistry test together. Then we are going for play tryouts. I am hosting a surprise birthday party for Rikki at my house (except that it's not a surprise). We complain about our math homework. We walk home from school together. We talk, we laugh, we dream together.

I am suddenly transported *there*, back to my old house, my old school. I am happier and more alive than ever.

My happy thoughts make for a happy mind, a happy me.

They say happiness is in the state of mind.

Is it really all up to me?

❋ ❋ ❋

I ACCOMPANY RIKKI to the airport, as if that "one last hour" and "one last minute" really help. I wave and wave till my hand aches. Goodbye, Rikki. Hello, reality.

Chapter Eight

February

It is one of those days. Everything is just so hard, so different, so lonely. It is only three thirty in the afternoon, and a long, empty day yawns ahead. I've become Israeli enough to change my clothes when I come home from school — why, there's still a long day left! No one stays in her uniform.

But now, the day is too long. I am bored and lonely, and this feeling scares me. Me, bored? I was always busy, way too busy. Busy with school, busy with tests, busy with homework, busy with friends, busy with play practice. But busy me is now bored me.

The afternoon drags on, and I watch the sun slowly disappear. The world is now dark, like my mood.

Good ol' sis Chaya hears my voice on the phone and gets right to it. "Malka, you're down in the dumps today, right?"

My silence is her answer.

"How would you like life to be right now?" she asks. "What can you do to help yourself?"

I have nothing to say.

"What can we change?" she persists.

Change? I want to change everything, but I can change nothing.

"There's life, and there's you. Guess which one we can change."

She's funny, Chaya.

"Good, you're laughing. So let's stay positive now. Think of three good things you gained by moving to Israel."

What did I gain?

Deep breath.

One: I am in the Holy Land, Hashem's land. It is a mitzvah to live here. I am closer to Hashem than before. That's one.

I am learning to live with challenge, and hopefully, to overcome it…eventually. I am gaining maturity and the ability to deal with something that is not all peaches and cream. That's two.

I am learning sensitivity. I know the feeling now of being a newcomer, and I am more sensitive to others' feelings because of it. I find that I am able to detect when someone's feeling down or lonely, and when that is the case, I try to make a point of cheering the person up. I know it's important — oh, how I know! That's three.

Uh...did she say three? There's more. I am becoming more self-aware. I am experiencing my world of thoughts and emotions more deeply. I am moving inward, instead of only living on the outside front. Four.

I am becoming more understanding and accepting of others. I understand that if I am different from everyone else, and that's okay, then others may be different from me, and that's okay, too. Five.

And hey! I am becoming creative, searching for solutions to making myself happy. Six!

How's that for a happier day?

"Happiness is in the state of mind" is transformed into a merry poster above my bed. I have fun cutting and pasting orange and yellow letters onto red cardboard paper, and wow, my room looks real cheery!

I find myself thinking of that poster all the time. I think of it when my class is singing a song I can't catch onto for the life of me. And when, during recess, I have to muster up the courage to go and talk to someone. And when I'm missing a grand Shabbaton with my old friends...

One good thing leads to the next, and finally, I find myself a friend: a trusty journal!

Page 1: Only in Israel

"*Pitot! Pitot!*" A dark-skinned man waves a bag of fresh pitas.

"*Tzedakah, tzedakah...Rachmanim bnei Rachmanim...*" a bent-over woman begs, shaking her *tzedakah* box.

I am surrounded by Jews, Jews, and more Jews. Jews so diverse, but all with one heart full of love for the Kosel.

A security guard opens my purse, gives a half-hearted peek inside, and waves me off. These Israelis are shrewd. They don't waste time checking out innocent people like me. They say Israeli security officials test you by looking you in the eye, not in your purse. They know the look of evil too well.

I reach the ancient stones. They are familiar to me by now, and so comforting. They are my old friend in the absence of a human one. Here I feel so connected, so safe.

Only in Israel.

❋ ❋ ❋

It could be a Gemara *shiur*, but it is actually just an ordinary bus ride in Yerushalayim. The bus driver and a *Chassidishe* man are arguing over the true meaning of a Gemara. But there is not enough time. The *Chassidishe* passenger has to get off.

"Ask your *rav*; you'll see I'm right!" the chassid calls as he steps off the bus.

"Okay, *yedidi* (my friend)!" the driver says.

Sometimes we argue, and sometimes we agree. But we are always friends.

Only in Israel!

❋ ❋ ❋

It's the third time someone stops me to say that I need a coat. It is raining and cold, but I left the house when it was warm and sunny. Everyone is worried. The responses span from friendly to protective to angry.

"Mamme'le, you'll catch a cold like that!"

"*Yaldah*, you need a coat in this weather! Do you live close by so you can get a coat? Do you want to come to my house and get a coat? I live right down the block!"

"You can't leave your house like that! Where's your coat? Do you want to get sick?!"

It's not just a feeling; I am really everyone's daughter and everyone's sister.

Only in Israel!

✹ ✹ ✹

LEARNING HEBREW is far more than learning the words and knowing how to construct a sentence. Hebrew is a language of the spirit, and that takes time to learn. "*Be'ezrat Hashem* (with Hashem's help)" must precede or end almost every sentence.

In Israel, more so than anywhere else, Hashem is in the heart. Hashem is in the mind. And Hashem is on your lips.

✹ ✹ ✹

GEVERET CHADAD, my *Sephardi* neighbor, always complains to me that the neighbors in our apartment building don't make periodical get-togethers on Shabbos or Rosh Chodesh.

"Neighbors have to be friends!" she maintains.

Geveret Chadad gets angry if anyone violates that rule. She got so offended when I once returned an egg to her that I had borrowed, exclaiming, "You think I can't give you an egg once, *neshamah*?! You're embarrassing me!"

Only in Israel!

✸ ✸ ✸

Geveret Shachar from the first floor is always dusted with flour or cocoa. She loves what she bakes — and so do I!

Yesterday she made rugalach; today it is pinwheel cookies. A sample of her day's creations is always waiting for me at my door, along with the yummy aroma that wafts from her apartment. "Taste it! Taste it!" is her frequent refrain.

It sure makes life here real yummy!

✸ ✸ ✸

I get inspiration from bumper stickers, store awnings, and door nameplates, to name just a few. Everything shouts, *"B'Shem Hashem na'aseh v'natzliach!* (With the Name of Hashem we will accomplish and succeed!)" or *"Ein od milvado*! (There is none other besides Him!)"

Only in Israel!

✸ ✸ ✸

Torah is the spoken language in Israel. A neighbor posts a *hashavas aveidah* notice that he found some bills in the building lobby. This tiny square note is quickly filled with halachic arguments over the next few days by different neighbors: *Isn't this something without identifying marks, which means it doesn't have to be returned? This is* reshus harabim *(public domain)! No, an apartment building with this amount of residents is not a reshus harabim.* More quotes from Gemara and *Chazal* that I can't decipher are scrawled on every empty corner of the note. I don't know what the resolution is, but I sure know this happens only in Israel!

✼ ✼ ✼

I THINK OUR CLEANING LADY, Dalia, could make a good *rebbetzin*. "*Mi'Shamayim* (from Heaven)" is her answer to almost anything.

We need her an hour less this week? "*Parnassah mi'Shamayim!*"

It rained right after she cleaned the windows? "*Mi'Shamayim!*"

She missed her bus home? "It's *mi'Shamayim!*"

The Heavens are so close in Israel. You just have to reach up, and you can touch them.

Only in Israel.

Chapter Nine

March

The land of Israel is a study in contrasts. In the North it's cold, but just two hours away, the weather is a free sauna. You have bustling, crowded cities with *sabras* all over each other, and then there are calm, country-like villages just fifteen minutes away from that. *Moshavim* dot the landscape of Israel, and they are like long swigs of cold water in the midst of a sweaty marathon.

For a field trip, my teacher takes our class to her town, which is actually a farm town. Yup, she lives on Moshav Kommemiyut. But as we tour the place, I see it's more than a farm; it's a farm with a soul. The people there have their cows and chickens and corn and cucumbers — but above all, they have the Torah.

I witness self-sufficiency at its best: produced in this farm are fresh eggs and milk (creamy, they say, nothing like what you've ever tasted), corn, cucumbers, tomatoes, and much more.

The cows, goats, and chickens seem friendly enough, nice and Jewish. The farmers patiently explain to us how eggs are hatched, and the process involved in egg distribution, from when the chickens lay eggs until those eggs are in cartons at our corner grocery. I watch boys half my age agilely milking cows over pails. A part of me tells me that this is really what life is all about: working for your food, for your existence. *Moshav* life says, "Do it yourself!"

An open truck roars toward us, and the driver jumps out, calling for us to hop on. He can't wait to show us around the fields of Kommemiyut.

The wind whips at our faces as the driver shouts and points: Here are the corn fields! There, to your right! Down there we grow peppers, yes, all of them, red, orange, yellow, green! There are the cabbage plants, see? Yup, straight ahead! Fresh and crunchy! Look at Hashem's beautiful food! We think *we* grow the vegetables, but no, we don't! Could I ever make such a beautiful pepper? Could you? He grows the plants, only He!

And the smile on his face is bright, as the sun's smile from above.

We soon settle in a circle on the grass for a country-style brunch with freshly plucked vegetables, courtesy of Kommemiyut. There is something deliciously enticing about cutting up a pepper that was attached to the ground just minutes ago. It is a slice of earth and heaven in the same bite. As I chew, I feel Hashem's love entering my bloodstream, while the sun right above the open field hugs me tight.

A born-and-bred New Yorker, I feel especially fortunate to enjoy the miracle of nature. How many stations did my peppers go through, back in smoky New York, and how long did passing through all those stations take? In contrast to that, any city in Israel is not too far from a *moshav*, and produce arrives fast. Here we are lucky to have our meals served up fresh every day, straight from Hashem's kitchen.

The *moshav* experience is complete. My classmates and I play catch on the grass, laughing like little girls, and then take turns jumping on our teacher's huge trampoline in her yard. Backyards are rare in Israel's cities, but in the *moshav* everyone has one, complete with picnic tables and chairs, swings, and other kiddie delights.

I sniff in the fresh country air and sigh happily. Contentment in the *moshav* is out here for the taking, and I am grateful for every bit.

Chapter Ten

March

Welcome to second grade. I almost expect that to be posted on the classroom door. Except that this is twelfth grade.

I am reading a paragraph aloud: "Sima opened the door and said hello. And they lived happily ever after."

"Good!" Mrs. Freilich says to me with a knowing wink.

Now I have to answer the question on the bottom of the page: *What did Sima say after she opened the door?*

Duh. Now, if you get the answer right, you get one point. If you get it right *and* spell it right, you get two. Uh...how do you spell hello?

I thought I'd be bored in English class, but I'm actually finding it interesting. English class is entertainment time. I sit back and relax and enjoy the show. But the rest of the class? They are not amused at all as they try hopelessly to decipher an unfriendly language.

They're lucky they have me. And you know what? I'm lucky now that I have them. How else would I have friends, if not for English class?

After class there is a desperate clamor around my desk.

"You must help me with grammar homework!"

"Please, can you study with me for the test next week?"

"Can you fix up this sentence for me?"

"Can you look over my project before I hand it in?"

I'm glad to help out. I'm even gladder to be useful. And even gladder to have friends.

By the time recess is over, there is a tottering pile of papers cluttering my desk. Meet Malka, the in-house tutor. I'm grateful for the job.

But I'd love to have a *real* friend. Oh, how I wish! For now, though, this is better than nothing.

During breaks, I keep myself busy correcting sentences, reading over papers, revising, commenting on compositions (that remind me fondly of mine back in third grade), and fixing spelling mistakes.

In the afternoons, I sit hunched over my dining room table with a few desperate girls, helping them with vocabulary lists and grammar homework. We have a laugh when, during English class one day, I discover that I haven't done my own homework (really, three minutes — at most — on a hard day) after having helped almost the entire class with theirs.

On the day before an English test, I have a full-time job. My dining room is converted into a classroom, with a huge oaktag hung on the wall as the board, and I am the teacher, tutor, and waitress all rolled into one. At eleven o'clock at night, I clear away a jumble of pens, pencils, and erasers, and pieces of leftover popcorn scattered all over the table.

I think Mrs. Freilich is secretly happy I'm doing a fair share of her work. I should really get a salary.

Nah, forget about the salary. A little friendship is reward enough.

Yet I have learned what real friends are all about. Friendship is precious and rare. That's not only a cliché.

What does it take to make a real friend? A lot.

Many hours spent poring over books and homework sheets still can't do the trick. Things like trust, candor, and interest can. If I would've opened my heart, if they would've…but we didn't.

Friendship takes over a part of your heart, and it takes courage to give that part up. I'm not ready to give a piece of myself to just anyone.

Oh, how much more I appreciate my old friends now. I know I must hold on to them tightly, tie their hands to mine, so I know I have them forever. For I don't know if I will have other friends like them.

I *cannot* ever have another friend like my old friends. How could a new friendship ever compare to the intensity and trust of a friendship cultivated since toddlerhood? Could anyone be so close to my heart as one who went through the joys and throes of fifteen years together with me? As one who saw me through tests, and fights, and homework, and punishments, and graduations — and stayed with me?

A childhood friend is yours, and yours forever.

✸ ✸ ✸

I AM LEARNING ENGLISH! Yes, surprise, surprise! I am learning English in Israel. Did you know there are three kinds of "if's"? Or that there are a plethora of tenses in the English language? The past tense is much more than one tense — your fellow Israelis will tell you that. There is past simple, past progressive, past perfect. And — get this: there is *future past*! Do you know that there is a fundamental and essential difference between "she sits" and "she is sitting"? Don't you *dare* confuse them!

Now I know why most of my Israeli friends won't open their mouths in English. Can you imagine thinking before every sentence, *Now, which of the four possible tenses should this word be? Should it be past simple, past progressive, past perfect, future past…* By then you'd have forgotten what you wanted to say.

But I crave to learn *real* English. Oh, what I'd do to analyze a good English poem, or even to just write a book report!

But, sorry, no one here can appreciate anything more than, "The cat is fat. Run, cat, run." Well…almost.

If not English literature, I can enjoy the Hebrew literature we learn. My love of literature lets me stretch that far. And you know what? I really do enjoy it. The poems are exquisitely written, the prose articulate and meaningful. Literature is a trove of treasures — even in Hebrew.

Especially in Hebrew. Hebrew is based on the real language, culled from the mouth of the Creator Himself. Its words have unmatched profundity; its expressions are unbelievably poignant. I need no convincing about that.

✼ ✼ ✼

I MAY ONLY BE SEVENTEEN, but I already have a job. As the American newcomer in the neighborhood, and with time on my hands (no younger siblings to bathe at night), I am besieged with offers — no, demands. I must tutor my neighbors' — and neighbors' neighbors' — kids who are struggling with English, and that's a given. I'm not really given a choice.

Not that I mind. It sounds like a productive way to fill my time and my wallet. But I want to do my job well. I ask some experienced tutors for advice, and soon I am shopping for flashcards, stickers, and some other stuff I can't even name. I'm not the artistic type — my sketches of people are stick figures only — but other people are, and my little and big charges will need the hands-on stimulation.

Five o'clock p.m. finds me at my dining room table with a pile of colorful supplies and a shy student. All appears to be in order — and yet I am baffled. Here I'm teaching the ABC's with lots of visual stimulation, and my eight-year-old charge is actually cooperating, but *I* am getting bored. Frankly, I'm not all that interested in teaching the ABC's. I don't mind making the few dollars an hour, and I do like seeing a kid's face light up when understanding dawns, but that's about it. Maybe I would enjoy teaching a poem, but not "A is for apple." At the third session, I'm already wondering what in the world made me do this.

Well, I do know. Everyone assumed I'd make an excellent English tutor, and thus, so did I. But since when does *knowing* something mean that you can go ahead and *teach* it? A hefty dose of talent and interest in teaching is probably just as important.

I spend each forty-five-minute session peeking at my watch way too many times, until I finally get myself out of the job. I accept that I don't love flashing ABC cards, and that's okay.

❋ ❋ ❋

Color war is a flash of color in a rainy, gray winter.

But this is no war of colors. This is a war of ideology, of principle!

The opposing teams are *Chutz* (Outside) and *Pnim* (Inside). Should you be on the outer front or in the inner bastion of *Yiddishkeit*? Inspire others or cultivate your inner world? Step out to change the world or stay inside to fend off unwanted influences?

Open *sefarim* and find out. Prove it! Quote it! Win it!

Forget soccer competitions and cheering, "We are the best; we're better than the rest!" Here you gotta *really* defend your team.

Israel, ever the land of the spirit.

The class splits up into groups of seven. One will write up an inspiring theme song, another will prepare convincing arguments for a live debate in the school auditorium, another will take care of the props for a live presentation, and the last group will perform the skit.

I can choose which group I want to join. But I don't want to join any. I am happy to be a spectator, as always since I moved here. I don't join a group, and no one notices.

Competition is fierce. I walk into the school building on presentation day and bump into a massive globe turning on its axis (how, pray tell?). Huge lettering on it screams out: *YOU can change the world!* Travel brochures are ready on a stand nearby.

I am still recovering from the bash on my nose when I feel a sense of warmth enveloping me. I look ahead, and there is a fireplace crackling away, with a beautifully designed sign near it inviting everyone to, *Come in! It's warm inside.* A girl taps me on the shoulder and offers me hot cocoa, urging me to sit on the specially prepared benches near the fireplace with some more cocoa-sipping girls.

Pesukim and *ma'amarei Chazal* adorn the walls everywhere. *B'shvili nivra ha'olam* — "The world was created for me." *U'k'she'ani l'atzmi, mah ani* — "When I am for myself, what am I?"

The live debate tingles my brain, feeding it a jumble of opinions and sources that it will have to slowly sort through. This color war is straining my mind, not my vocal cords. In this competition, you don't scream you're the best; you prove it with real arguments. You don't want to win for winning's sake; you want to win your pursuit of truth.

Reading material is thrown everyone's way. *Parshah* insights, short stories, and cartoons convince you, inform you, inspire you.

As I delve into another deep argument about one's power to change the world, I think back to the wild cheering campaigns of the American-style color wars I've participated in, and I realize I have crossed more than just a few continents. I've come to a new world of thought.

Israel is a study in itself, with a thesis that is entirely different from anywhere else. It has its own vocabulary, its own edition of dictionary definitions.

Even fun has a whole different meaning here.

Chapter Eleven

March

This year I dress up on Purim — as an Israeli girl! Looking at myself in the mirror, I must admit that I've come a long way, if you'd put it that way, since I moved here. Israeli norms have influenced me, for better or for worse, and sometimes I'm shocked at how...*Israeli* I look!

The real costumes, though, are my nieces' and nephews', of course. I've had fun buying and matching, fixing and cutting. I think deep inside every *frum* teenager and adult is a child whose highlight on Purim is the costumes. Does anyone really ever outgrow that?

This year, we will finally celebrate Purim with a crowded table and a huge *seudah* challah, and I can't wait. For years we'd dreamed of this, and finally the big Purim reunion with my married siblings has come. Thanks, Israel!

April

THERE ARE SOME TIMES when only family will do, and no matter how many friends you have, you will need family. One such time is the Pesach Seder. Back in the States, I was quite lonely on Pesach when my married siblings didn't come from Israel. The Seder seemed too short, and Chol Hamoed seemed too long.

Now, I cannot wait for Pesach. I finish cleaning my room way in advance, and for the full two weeks of vacation before Pesach, I go to help my sisters. I am overwhelmed by the galaxy of work there is to be done in a house full of kids, and most days I just end up sleeping over. I crouch near the refrigerator and scrub away, and then wash down baby carriages on the porch under the Israeli sun.

One day, my sister and I roll up our sleeves and paint the dining room. Yup, we paint it all by ourselves. Israeli society sure is economical, and painting your walls is as ordinary as washing them — or even more common (it's easier to paint on top of the cheap paint than to scrub it!). We climb up on ladders, turn up the music, and get our rollers going. And hey, for someone who messed up with every painting project in elementary school, I'm doing a pretty good job! I'm surprised and thrilled when I finally survey the freshly redone dining room.

Erev Pesach is the perfect opportunity to learn to do Sponja, capital S, please. Any self-respecting Israeli must do a good sponja. Basically, the talent involves cleaning your floor so people can actually lick it (yes, that's the no-frills way of defining it). I'm pretty disappointed after my first try, though, because I'm not too tempted to lick the floor I just sponja-ed. My sister consoles me that it's just a matter of time until I'll get it right.

It's a science, this sponja thing: First you swish a dripping rag over the floor and spill some more soapy water from the bucket for good measure. Then you aggressively sweep up the water with a sponja stick into the hole in the bathroom (it's covered otherwise, don't worry). Then you wipe down the whole floor with a damp rag. Now *that's* what Israelis call clean!

WHEN THE SEDER finally arrives, I am tired but elated. This year we celebrate it in style — *all* my married siblings come, in honor of our first Pesach living in Israel. And I'd better enjoy every minute of it — there's only one Seder this year! It feels strange to pick up the telephone just a night after the Seder — why, is Yom Tov over already? But too soon, the day after Shevi'i Shel Pesach, it doesn't even feel funny to eat *chametz*, because everyone else is doing it — that's how fast it takes to get used to one day of Yom Tov. Yup, what *everybody* does really does make a difference!

Instead of riding roller coasters this Chol Hamoed, I visit extended family. One day we visit a great-aunt, and another day we travel to our cousins, and it is fun! It isn't the screeching thrill of an amusement park, but it is the satisfaction of connecting with your flesh and blood, even if they are of different types and stripes. I find that here, Chol Hamoed morning doesn't begin with, "What are we doing today?" The day is centered around a lavish Yom Tov meal and then visits to family, the Kosel, and *talmidei chachamim* or *rebbes* for the boys. Each day is fulfilling and joyful, true to the spirit of Yom Tov.

The end of Pesach leaves me feeling joy and dejection at the same time. It was such a beautiful Yom Tov...I'm already waiting impatiently for next Pesach!

✿ ✿ ✿

May

TODAY IS LAG B'OMER, and we're on our way, my big sisters, Chaya and Nechama, and I, up, up, up to Meron.

Drinks, drinks, and more drinks. I watch carton after carton pile up in the trunk of the bus. Cola, Pepsi, orange juice, mango nectar — you name it. Countless hands busily pack in more and more containers of drinks. It's the *segulah* of *Chai Rotel*, the ritual of distributing a large amount of drinks to thirsty visitors in Meron on Lag B'Omer, for the *zechus* of a *yeshuah*.

My bag is bulging with three water bottles and a load of snacks, and an apple sneaked in by my mother at the last minute, for a three a.m. feast. Chaya, Nechama, and I clamber onto the bus, sitting down in the last three empty seats.

"*Amar Rabi Akiva...v'ahavta l're'acha kamocha...*" Strains of lively music compete with a babble of excited voices. There are first-timers and old-timers on the bus, well-prepared women alongside wide-eyed preteens hardly believing their good fortune in coming along. I don't know who is more excited.

I am tired, but I cannot sleep. The thrill, the adventure, the togetherness, and the prayer on this bus are electrifying. Everyone pins their hopes on the magical day of Lag B'Omer.

The engine sputters, and the bus zooms off. We are on our way. Corn chips, anyone?

The woman sitting in front of us promptly opens her *Tehillim*, and only closes it three and a half hours later, when we finally step out into the northern chill. And that is only a prelude to another hour of praying at the *tziyun* of Rabi Shimon Bar Yochai. It's like her whole world depends on her *tefillos*. It does — and so does mine.

The *tziyun* that can normally accommodate one hundred and fifty people packs in now about six hundred. I cannot move my hand to get my siddur from my bag. How am I to *daven* this way?

So I *daven* without a siddur. With my mouth. With my soul. I beg. I cry. I learn from everyone around me. No one is embarrassed. So many tears, so many tissues.

I feel a little sad. Do you need to come all the way to Meron to be moved to tearful prayers? There must be a way to do that back home.

A few lucky women stand at the grave itself. I try to inch forward; maybe, just maybe, I can come a bit closer… But instead of coming closer, I fall backward, slamming into the woman behind me.

So I will pray from wherever I am. I shut my eyes, overwhelmed by the blaring band and singing voices coming from the men. Everyone is so happy, and so tearful.

* * *

IT'S A FEW WEEKS LATER, and I'm back up in the heights, in Tzfas, on a family trip, amid the great people of yesteryear. The tzaddikim I learned about in Jewish history are all here — to my right, to my left, wherever I turn. I can start Shacharis at the grave of Rabi Pinchas ben Yair, continue near Rabi Shlomo Alkabetz, and finish at the Alshich's side.

The air is brisk and sharp. It is only seven in the morning, but people are out and about. In the mystical city of Tzfas, everyone's too busy praying to sleep.

"Here," my sister Chaya points, "are the fields where, it is said, the Arizal would go out and sing *Lecha Dodi*, to welcome the Shabbos."

I close my eyes, imagining groups of saintly Jews with flowing robes, arms outstretched to the pinkish-purple sky, singing a haunting, yearning tune. "*Lecha Dodi likras kallah.* Go, my Beloved One, toward the Shabbos bride..."

We finish *davening* and then make the trek to the city. Up and down, up and down. Tzfas doesn't sit still.

The Old City of Tzfas beckons. It is fresh with promise as much as it is old. I tour the narrow streets, still paved with cobblestones, with a groove in the middle for horses to trot. Arched doorways welcome me into art shops and souvenir boutiques.

A long-bearded artist proudly displays his latest work of art: the words of *Az Yashir* written in tiny letters forming a painstaking illustration of the Splitting of the Sea. I wonder how much he works for the money and how much for himself.

Next, we stop by the shul of the Arizal. People pray there today. I wonder if life is different when the past is such a bold part of your everyday existence. What is it like, to tread the same path as the greats of yesteryear?

Eretz Yisrael, the land of yesterday, today…and tomorrow.

Chapter Twelve

June

" cheese!"

I try.

"No, your smile has to be natural, but also formal. Not too bright, but not too tight."

Hmmph. I try again.

Flash!

Into the yearbook I go.

My old friends had encouraged me to get my picture taken, so I could be entered into their twelfth-grade yearbook. Acting on their advice, I got my hair done and went, all alone, to the photographer's studio, to have my picture taken and then submitted for my old class's yearbook, as if I'm there with them. As if I'm finishing high school with them. As if nothing changed.

I am happy but self-conscious as I pose for the picture. Am I part of them, or not part of them?

Has the year that I've been here changed me to an unrecognizable degree? Am I a different person than the carefree girl who left the class back then? Is my smile the same? Do my eyes have the familiar twinkle? Is my expression unchanged?

Am I my old self? Will my old friends recognize me?

I look at the picture before sending it off, and I see myself. A changed self. Whether I like it or not, I've changed. And I think I like it.

Three cheers! I said it. I like it. I'm happy I'm here. I'm happy. I'm happy. I'm really happy!

But I'm also sad. I'm sad I'll be missing the grand Catskills Shabbaton in honor of graduation. The fun, the adventure, the togetherness...I'll be missing all that. I keep tabs on the goings-on before the big trip, and I'm even sadder. Chana is writing the theme song, Devora and Sury are doing the comedy, Henny is preparing the *dvar Torah*... And me? And me? And me????

I will write them a letter.

Dear (former?) classmates,

Hi, everyone! With some of you I've only chatted yesterday; with some I haven't spoken in a year. Yes, a whole year! But I miss you. Believe me that I miss you, even if I haven't called you all this time. I remember the smile on your lips and in your eyes. I know your favorite food and your worst subject. I could imagine the expression on your face when you read this letter.

But still, I don't know what you're thinking. I don't know if you're thinking — about me, that is — at all. I'm not sure if you know I miss you. But I'm also not sure if it means that much to you. Perhaps I'm just a wisp of a memory for you, a feather fluttering in the recesses of your brain. Perhaps my absence means for you that I don't exist. But you are alive for me, real people who I care about deeply. I hear your voices and see your faces. I can almost imagine that I am talking to you.

I'll say it again: I miss you. But do you remember me?

Forever your friend,
Malka

I won't send this letter. It is written with tears and pain, and it must remain mine. Do the others care that I'm not part of their fun? Or have they forgotten all about me? Is life any different for them since I'm gone? Or am I the only one grieving?

I am afraid to hear the answer.

Those gone are quickly forgotten, but those who go never forget.

It is painful, but it is the truth.

It is time. It is time to move beyond the past; time for me to find a life for myself, here, in the present. Life is not an exclusive New York commodity; it is the privilege of every human being on this planet.

I just have to find my way to express it, here, in the moment, on the shores of Eretz Yisrael.

Oh, it is hard to let go and move on, to admit that this is my life. My past and I...we are intertwined. It is a part of me, and I am a part of it. How can you separate the two of us?

But do we have to separate? No. Do I have to live in the present in spite of it? Yes. I can allow my past only so much space in me, and then I must say, *That's it. The rest belongs to the moment.*

I *can* keep my past. I don't have to abandon it. I never have to fear — my past will always remain mine. My memories are stored neatly inside, and I can pull out pictures as I please. But I must always put them back afterward.

And live the moment.

The moment? It is an exciting moment. Mazel tov! My first Israeli classmate is engaged!

It is a first, and we have to do it right. At seven o'clock sharp the next morning, we are all in school, hard at work on huge, colorful "mazel tov" posters. We hang them at the school entrance, on our classroom door, and on the classroom walls. Everyone is so excited; we're almost embarrassed to show just how much.

An engagement! What's it like to be engaged? Has Menucha grown since last night? Is she bigger and better than the rest of us?

We cannot wait to find out.

Menucha is ushered in with song, dance, hugs, and kisses. She is glowing. We swirl around her in raucous circles in the lobby, drunk with excitement. I catch a glimpse of a glittering bracelet peeking out from under Menucha's sleeve. It is real. It is *kallah* time!

A line of girls form to wish Menucha mazel tov. She wishes everyone, "*B'karov etzlech* (may it be soon by you)," and privately, everyone must be wondering just how soon their turn will come.

Menucha invites the class over for Shabbos afternoon, for a celebration. She serves some cake and drinks, but most of the time, we (I mean *they*; no, I don't sing Israeli songs with Israelis) sing, and sing, and sing, all the way from stirring, tear-jerking songs to lively ones, accompanied by effusive dancing.

Finally, Shabbos is over and we all leave, a smile on our lips and a dream in our hearts.

But life must go on! The year is drawing to a close. There are things to wrap up, or better said, tests to take.

Chutzim (tests administered by the board of education) are the talk of the day. It's time to study, and study, and study. For weeks all I can think about is Napoleon, and radiation, and algebra equations. Will this ever end?

Piles of notebooks clutter my room, and when I'm lucky, a friend and her notebooks join, and sometimes some pizza, too, for good measure. Ode to pizza and falafel: You are the best; you help me pass my test!

There is another page, and another chapter, and then another ten exercises to practice. There is more, and more, and more. Sometimes I just close my eyes and think of the beach, and sand, and sky. When will summer come?

But it will come. Summer always comes after spring, doesn't it? Be patient, I tell myself; this season will pass.

I am finishing twelfth grade — yes, TWELFTH GRADE!

But could you guess?

Graduation? No. Yearbook? No. Trip? No. Party? No.

Forget about ceremony; there are another two years to go until graduation.

Welcome to grade five of high school. And grade six.

School in Israel stretches all the way until you're twenty, and yes, you can come to class in your *sheitel*. I picture going to school one day and then celebrating my wedding that night. And the next day, yes, I'm back in school, at eight o'clock sharp!

And how about graduating alongside lucky babies adorned in caps and gowns on their mothers' laps? "Me and my baby — we did it together!"

As the weeks go by, friends get engaged by the dozen (well, almost), and they have to make the agonizing decision of whether to stay in school or not. Do they want to become teachers and stick it out till the end, so they can get a diploma? Will they be able to pay tuition(!)? Is there a profession they can learn in school for a future career?

The future is uncertain, scary, promising, and exciting, all at the same time. Who knows what life has in store for us? But for now, I'll just take one day at a time.

And that includes — taking my sisters up on their offer for an impromptu, so-called "twelfth grade graduation trip"! I'm American, after all, and, lucky girl that I am, my big sisters don't want me to be deprived of something so basic to every twelfth grader in the U.S.A. So, the day that school is out, my sisters and I are off to the South for an overnight trip!

I never realized how salty salt is. I am floating on a warm bed of salt water, upon the Yam Hamelach, the Dead Sea. The sting in my eyes alarms me. I cry out, but my faint voice disappears in the air around me. I close my eyes, and I feel a bit better. I tip my face up to the sky and relax my body. The glare of the burning sun still blinds me, even with my eyes closed.

There are only a handful of people here today besides me and my sisters, and each minds her own business. One woman reads a book, another takes a tan, another sleeps in her beach chair.

The silence all around comforts me. It's me and the sky and the water, sandwiched into one. Here, in this lowest spot on earth, I feel high and closer to Heaven than ever.

The salt water is an obedient friend, not moving unless I move. Not the slightest ripple disturbs the serenity of the sea. It is placid, and so am I.

I step out of the water, tiptoeing on the rocky earth to find a beach chair. I recline comfortably, my swimming clothes drying quickly in the sun.

Soon enough, it is time to go, and then — on to the desert. Beige sand is all you see, whichever way you turn. Throw in some camels, and you have a perfect picture. Now, it's me and the sand and the sky, sandwiched into one.

I can understand why newcomers to Eretz Yisrael kissed the sand at their feet when they arrived. You see it, you experience it, you love it.

Chapter Thirteen

July

Soon, I will be on an airplane again.

I start packing my suitcase three weeks early. I check off the boxes on the countdown chart above my bed right after I wash *negel vasser.*

My plane ticket, carefully enclosed in an envelope, has rested on my dresser since the day I found it placed there by my father, as a birthday present for me.

It all started with a phone call. It seemed ordinary, at first. Rikki was on the line. She got straight to the point.

"Malka, you can't say no to this."

"No."

"Ha, ha. Okay, listen to this. Mrs. Simon called me yesterday."

"Mrs. Simon from Camp Binah?"

"Uh-huh. She asked me if I want to be the assistant play director this summer."

"Whoa!"

"Wait. You didn't hear the best part. She asked if I had any ideas of a girl I wanted to work with. And I thought of you."

"Ha, ha."

"No, really! This is the best idea. You're coming to camp for the summer!"

"You're…sponsoring my trip?"

"Noo…but this is the plan: You'll make a few hundred dollars on the play direction, right? Then add your few hundred from your savings. And…somehow you'll find a way to get the rest."

I was afraid to get excited. But two days after I had spoken to my parents, the ticket was ready on my dresser.

Thank you, Tatty!

I dig out the casual tee-shirts that weren't quite proper enough for Israeli apparel and stack them in my suitcase. Next go three pairs of sneakers that haven't been touched all year. Then I pile in my camera. Sunglasses. Cap.

Am I really going?

I am afraid to dream. Will all my wishes come true? Will my reunion with old friends be as exciting as I imagine it to be? Will visiting my old neighborhood be as exhilarating as my expectations?

But away with the dreams. There is no time. It's almost time to fly!

Finally, I stand alone in the airport, again. But I am not the same frightened, jittery girl glancing nervously around the place. I am not blinking back stubborn tears threatening to embarrass me.

I am a big girl, a strong girl. I have spanned continents on my own. I have braved a new climate, tested new, frigid waters. I've mastered a new tongue, including its puns and nuances. I have learned to expect less and accept more.

I sit back in my airplane seat, anxious for takeoff. I can't wait to whiz through the skies, watch the passing clouds, and let my thoughts soar along with the rest of me, to help me understand myself and the world under me.

The world is tiny now, but that's really the way it is, always. It is a tiny world, with tiny people, who have tiny lives. But I can try to make my tiny life into something big, bigger than this world, so that it reaches up to the skies.

The airplane is now on a steady track, moving forward, westward. But in a way, that is really backward. Who was it who said that his heart was always in the east?

Of course Rav Yehudah Halevi said it first, but the girl sitting right next to me is telling me the same thing. What are the chances for two *frum* girls to sit side by side on a packed airplane? We are both grateful for the opportunity to be together, and we schmooze.

At first she is timid, but I see she wants to talk. She tells me she is going to spend the summer with cousins in the United States, but she doesn't seem the least bit glad about it. Sadly, her mother passed away a half a year ago, and her father sent her to America to loosen up and have some fun. But there is no fun in her eyes, only mourning.

She can't believe she won't be at the Kosel on Tishah B'Av. She wants to sit on the stone floor there, like every year, and wail all night. But unlike every year, this year she has a mother to cry for, too.

We talk, and doze off, and nosh on chocolate bars together. We try some Sudoku puzzles and then talk some more. In the sky, it's easy to be friends. We plan to keep in touch, but I wonder if, when we stumble back into the buzz of real life again, we will remember that.

Still, it's okay to be friends for now. I can hold Naomi's hand tight, and listen to her, and help her wipe her tears. I can be a friend, even if it's just for now. And, after all, the sky's a private place. It's just me and Naomi and the clouds around us. Her feelings and her tears are safe.

We stay together, through landing, arrival, and the endless airport corridors we have to wind through — until we are both swept into embrace. She meets her aunt and cousins and I meet Rikki, and we say goodbye.

Rikki and her mother have it all prepared: American donuts and nutty chews are thrust into my hands. I am hungry, and I polish off the sweet treats that have an even sweeter taste of nostalgia to them.

Rikki is the same, her mother is the same. The donuts and nutty chews are the same. Only I, it seems, have changed.

But in the car, on the way "home," we are already babbling about our plans for the camp production, and it seems not much has changed after all. We are best friends with sometimes like, and sometimes different, opinions. We can poke fun at each other and then get serious again in seconds.

Friendship is forever, and that makes everything all right. Life is familiar, and we are familiar to each other. Some things always stay the same, and I am comforted.

※ ※ ※

CAMP IS STARTING in only two days. Rikki and I sit through the night, revising songs, planning with the pianist, coordinating sewing heads. It's almost like we are back in school, preparing for grand production.

We are off to camp, on a noisy coach bus, with old friends and some new ones. Everyone is spellbound about the story of a girl on a coach bus with unfamiliar faces, also on her way to "camp," Israeli-style. The view outside, when the story took place, was more breathtaking than the view from these windows, but the girl on that bus was feeling trapped and frightened, not delighted like she is feeling today.

My friends scrutinize me with curious wonder. Did you really go through all that? How? And you look the same! We'd never guess!

I smile mysteriously. Some things are inside, and if they're not said outright, no one could ever guess they're there.

✽ ✽ ✽

THE COUNTRY AIR is as brisk as I remembered it to be. Rikki and I stroll around the camp grounds, looking for the staff bunkhouse. Staff! The last time I was here, I was a senior, and now I am part of the staff. Growth spurt, isn't it? You'd better believe it. In more ways than one.

Everything is familiar. The camp office. Bunkhouses. Lunchroom. Canteen. But I feel strangely detached, like I knew this in another lifetime. I am not part of this, not really. I am not like the others here in camp. I am the visitor from Israel, back to entertain my buddies with my adventures in the Holy Land.

But no matter. I will have fun, anyway. And I will have even more fun when it is not tinged with the sadness and the hope of coming back. I am no longer a part of this American world, and I can never truly go back to it.

But you know what? I can say that without crying.

Chapter Fourteen

August

I chomp chewing gum furiously. The plane is landing, and my ears are clogged. Chew, chew, chew until your ear pops.

Aaaah…pop! We landed. A spirited applause breaks out on the plane. Good job, pilot!

The sun is bright, like it always is in Israel.

Déjà vu creeps up over me. This is a repeat of one year ago. Once again, I am starting anew.

A new chapter in life lies ahead. Seminary and *shidduchim* sweep me up in their fascinating arms.

A new school year is starting, but I feel confident and

independent. School is not the big, bad, scary guy anymore.

I am almost an adult.

※ ※ ※

SEMINARY IS FUN. The teachers who used to scold you like you were troublesome toddlers now smile at you like they're your equals. And the subjects — they're fresh and promising. Forget about history and math; that's for the kiddies. Now you learn psychology, methodology, *hashkafah*.

Ah, the newness of it all! It's a whole new life awaiting me, and I am awaiting it.

※ ※ ※

THERE IS A GIFT, and it's called the future. I am eager to unwrap it.

There's another gift, and that's the past. Sometimes I want to relive it.

But there's the greatest gift of all, and that's the present.

The End

Ahuva Talks:
Be My Pal

The pen-pal page of my favorite magazine, *Simcha*, always intrigued me. I loved seeing real names of real kids from out-of-town places. It was an exciting brush with reality: these were real kids in different places other than my school and my block! There was a Chany from Chicago, a Rochel from Miami, and a Bracha from Queens.

The names always looked so friendly, so inviting. *Write to me!* they seemed to say. *I want to be your friend.*

So one day I did. I chose Esty Abrams, fourteen years old like me, from Los Angeles. Los Angeles was far away and exciting.

Who knew; maybe if we'd become such good friends, I'd even fly there one day to visit this Esty!

I chose a pretty piece of stationery for my first letter and began to write:

Dear Esty,

I saw your name on the pen-pal list in *Simcha* magazine. Let me introduce myself. I'm Ahuva Silberman, from Flatbush. I am in the eighth grade in Bnos Miriam. I love making new friends, and I hope this will be the start of a friendship between us!

How is life in Los Angeles? I was never there, and I don't have any family there. Which school do you go to? Are you also in the eighth grade? How many girls are in your class?

Please write back!

Love,
Ahuva

I folded the letter and stuffed it into an envelope. I wrote the address carefully on the envelope and put a stamp in the corner. The letter was good to go. I went to the corner mailbox, dropped the letter in, and let it flutter...and fly miles away to Esty Abrams.

I couldn't wait for Esty's letter to arrive. I loved any letter addressed to me, even if it was only from the insurance company. It made me feel important and taken seriously, like I was an adult. I loved knowing that someone took the time to address something only to me.

It happened fast enough. The bright green envelope winked at me from the pile of boring white envelopes in the mailbox. I grabbed it and studied the outside: From Esty Abrams, to Ahuva Silberman. The envelope had actually been in this mysterious Esty Abram's house, in Los Angeles, and flown all the way to New York, right into my hands! It was a thrilling thought.

I tore open the envelope and began to read:

Dear Ahuva,

Thank you for your letter! I am excited to finally have a pen pal. There are only fifteen girls in my class — probably much less than in yours — so I'm always happy to "meet" new friends.

I am also in the eighth grade. My school is called Bais Devorah.

I'm on midwinter vacation now. Vacation in our school is for four days. When is your vacation?

Keep in touch,
Esty

By the time Pesach came around, Esty and I were great friends. We learned that we both loved reading, and our favorite subject was literature. We had our differences, too. That made things even more interesting. I shared instructions with her for how to make my favorite sandwich cookies, and she explained to me the difference between a guitar and a violin. She played the violin, and she must have done it really well, because she played for her school concert!

She also told me that she had twin baby brothers, and she knew all about diapering, feeding, and dressing babies. She was the oldest in the family and often babysat for her five brothers and sisters.

I was able to tell her all about what it's like to have your own room and have only one sister to fight with. I told her about my dream of becoming a first grade teacher and she supported me, telling me that she could just see me becoming the best one ever.

In some ways, she was a better friend than my best friends from school. Esty and I never had arguments, and we shared a lot of our inner lives. We sometimes shared things we wouldn't feel comfortable sharing in person.

Take the time my father fainted and went to the hospital. It was so scary; I didn't feel I could tell my friends about it and handle their reactions. The fear was too intense. When I wrote about it to Esty, though, it felt safer. From that distance, I felt I could let out my deepest fears and questions. *Baruch Hashem*, it turned out to be nothing serious, only a mild case of dehydration, but while we were unsure and afraid, I needed to tell somebody. Esty was the perfect address.

When Esty told me that she was going to Camp Achva in the summer, her letter literally dropped from my hands. I was going to Camp Achva, too! It was just too good to be true. We'd finally meet! I had no idea how Esty even looked. I had sent her my picture, but the one she'd sent me got lost in the mail, and she hadn't gotten around to sending another one yet.

One day, in the middle of math class, as I daydreamed about our upcoming "reunion," I had a brainstorm. I just couldn't wait to tell my mother. I counted down the hours till school would be over. When the dismissal bell rang, I took my schoolbag and ran all the way home. The delicious plan was just bursting on my lips.

"Ma, I have the best idea!" I blurted, puffing, as soon as I burst into the house.

"Oh, Ahuva, hello! You have an idea, all right! You've made it home in record time — it's four minutes on the clock since dismissal time."

"Yeah, I just had to tell you already! Look, Esty Abrams is coming to Camp Achva, right? I thought that it would be so much fun if she would come a day earlier from L.A. and sleep over at our house, so we could enjoy some time together. We'd pick her up from the airport, and maybe we could take her on a trip, or we could bake cookies together, or..."

"Hmmm, it does sound like fun. I'll ask Tatty."

When my father gave his okay that night, I whooped with delight. I ran to write another letter to Esty (we'd agreed not to talk on the phone; it was much more fun to be real pen pals!) and mailed it out right away.

Her letter came fast. She was just as excited as I was. She said she couldn't wait to see my frilly pink room, which I had told her all about, and to finally get to taste my famous sandwich cookies.

Tuesday morning, the day Esty was due to arrive, I was up bright and early, and chose my best outfit and headband. I smoothed the quilt cover on "Esty's" bed and rearranged the knickknacks on my shelf. I was all ready for Esty Abrams.

My mother and I climbed into a cab at eleven thirty in the morning and drove off to the airport. I looked out the window on the way, smiling to myself and thinking about the fun we would have.

We walked into the milling airport and searched for Esty. She was tall and dark-haired, she had told me. That was our only clue.

And then we met.

I looked at the tall, heavyset girl with rimless glasses and curly black hair that was pulled into a tight ponytail, and finally squeaked a nervous, "Hi." She looked at me and shyly said "Hi," too.

Nothing of the laughter and hugs and warm reunion I'd imagined.

She looked so different than I'd imagined. She was tall, very tall, and…heavy. I was a short, skinny kid. We made a real funny pair. She didn't look like as much fun as she sounded in her letters. She didn't look like the cute, creative girl I'd imagined her to be.

My stomach churned with butterflies. The whole thing was like a mean, horrible trick.

As my mother chattered to her about her flight, I saw her shoot nervous glances in my direction. I hadn't uttered one word other than that feeble "hi."

I opened my mouth, determined to try my best. "So…how was your flight?"

"Oh, it was fine. My mother's good friend was on the flight, too, and she sat next to me."

"Oh." I wanted to smile, but my mouth remained frozen.

Fortunately, we had to get going and start schlepping Esty's suitcases to the car, so we didn't have to stand around awkwardly anymore.

It felt good to help her with her bags. At least I was doing *something* nice.

The drive home was mostly silent, other than a few failed attempts at conversation.

We finally got home. After putting Esty's luggage in my room, we went downstairs to the kitchen and sat at the table. There was a plate of sandwich cookies in the middle of the table; I had placed it there before leaving to the airport.

"Umm, these are the cookies I told you about."

"You mean, wrote me about."

I tried to smile, but my mouth wouldn't budge. Why was my throat so dry? Why could I not bring myself to smile?

"So…take some."

Esty gingerly took a cookie off the plate, made a *brachah*, and finished it quickly, as if she were doing something wrong by eating it. She tried to avoid my gaze and kept herself busy looking around the kitchen.

My mother walked in then — just in time to save us.

"Girls, don't you want to take a picture together? This is something you're going to want to remember!"

"Okay," I said.

My mother got the camera and we went to the couch to pose for the picture. We sat down awkwardly, leaving a large space between us, and smiled at the camera, both of us stiff as tree barks.

"Arms over each other's shoulders," my mother chided, wagging a finger at us playfully.

I gulped. What way was it, really, to pose for a picture and keep your hands to yourself?

I took a deep breath and placed my arm around Esty's shoulder. She did the same, and it seemed like we were both holding our breaths until the camera flashed. Was I imagining it, or was there a mutual sigh of relief when the torturous hugging pose was over?

We were embarrassed to meet each other's eyes afterward. We had put our arms around each other's shoulders without having wanted to.

The day somehow passed. I showed Esti some of my school albums, and we ate my mother's delicious dinner.

We went to bed at nine thirty sharp. I don't remember ever going to sleep so early on a sleepover.

My dreams that night were very different from the ones I'd had the night before. The smiling girls of the night before now had sad faces. Esty Abrams wasn't the same pen pal I'd known from her letters. She just wasn't for me.

The next day was, fortunately, a busy one. We were scheduled to be at the bus stop for camp at twelve o'clock. We had to *daven*, eat, buy some goodies for the bus, and pack some last-minute things before then.

Twelve o'clock came fast enough. We stood at the bus stop with hundreds of other girls, all clutching overstuffed duffel bags and backpacks. I spotted some old camp friends — this was my third year going to Camp Achva, so I already had a *"chevrah"* of my own — and ran over to them.

Ouch. I'd left Esty behind. This was Esty's first year of camp, I knew, and she didn't know any of the girls there.

I ignored the guilty pang I felt and exchanged yelps of glee with my friends. We were so excited to meet again.

When I walked back to Esty (it wasn't hard to find her; she

towered over everyone), I experienced a bitter taste of regret. She looked sad. Not only was I being so unfriendly, I didn't even have the decency to introduce her to my friends.

Camp started out as fun as I always remembered it to be. As soon as we arrived there, the first thing we did was rush to the bunkhouses so we could catch good beds. I ran, along with everyone else, and so did Esty — but we didn't choose beds in the same room. I chose a top bunk, with my best camp friend, Rivka Schon, sleeping underneath. Now I was surrounded by my own familiar friends. I could finally breathe a sigh of relief. Esty was in a different room, and we didn't have to force ourselves to be friends anymore.

Although we kept our distance from each other, I always watched Esty carefully, curious to see how she'd adjust to camp.

It didn't take long for everyone to discover that Esty was the kindest and most talented girl in our age group. She always had the smartest things to say, and knew how to make everyone feel good. She was really special.

The counselors caught on to that, too, and they knew to choose her to say a *dvar Torah* on Shabbos for the whole camp, and to give her one of the leading parts in the camp play.

Esty made many friends; she was doing fine without me.

But suddenly, I wanted her.

I wanted to get to know her better and be her friend. I didn't only see her dress size anymore. I could see now that there was so much beyond that.

But it seemed that I'd opened my eyes too late. Camp was just about over. We were going to board the bus home in just two hours. Did I still have a chance?

As I stood with a crowd of girls waiting for the bus, I heard someone ask Esty, "Wasn't this was your first year in Camp Achva? Did you know anyone before?"

This was the moment.

I walked over to Esty, my heart in my mouth. "Yes, we were friends before. The best of pals...right?" Tentatively, I put my arm around her shoulder. "Pen pals!"

Esty looked at me and smiled. She put her arm around my shoulder, too, and the gesture was firm and full of warmth.

"We sure were. Keep in touch, Ahuva!"

Penina Talks:
BRAINS

I am the smartest kid in the class.

Big shot, huh? Well, let me just tell you this: I'm not always so thrilled about my status.

I sit in the back corner of the class, pushed near the coat hooks. Sometimes the coats even block my view. But after all, I get everything in a jiffy; I can handle getting lost in the corner.

Don't get me wrong. It's not always that bad. The back seat does offer many exclusive advantages. Like, you can do math homework in the middle of science — especially when your teacher is defining chlorophyll for the third time. You can also share a few whispers with a friend and, *l'havdil*, get in a *perek* of Tehillim when you're really desperate.

But still, it gets kind of lonely with hardly more than two walls for company, when my teacher looks at everyone else but me. Listen up, buddies, also smart kids need attention. More than you think. What's a brain got to do with a heart?

But I'm a confident kid, and from time to time I'll make it loud and clear that I exist. My heyday is when our *hashkafah* teacher brings up a topic for debate. Like, how can we look at *tznius* as a privilege instead of a burden? Then I get up and formulate a loud speech right on the spot, and everyone's like: *wow*. And I'm like, it's time you realized I'm here, stuck in the sleeve of your coat. Finally, mission accomplished.

When test time comes around, I really gotta roll up my sleeves. I don't need to study, right. So it's only fair that I help everyone else study. That's the common assumption.

Full disclosure: I *do* need to study. So thanks for saving my dignity, dear classmates. I'd be mortified for you to find out I'd been *studying* and not ice skating the night before a test. So here, you ask me for my help, and I get my studying in like that! If you think it's because of *me* that you passed the test, it's because of *you* that I did, too! Just because I get things quickly doesn't mean that my brain's a copy machine.

But hey, I'm getting ahead of myself. There's still a whole lot to do before we study for a test. First, I lend my notes to every single girl in the class (actually, I only lend them to the first girl, and then they make their rounds on their own) so they can photocopy them, and I finally get my notes back crumpled and creased, with some ketchup stains thrown in for the fun of it.

Once, in tenth grade, I spotted a group of ninth graders huddled over something in the middle of the hallway, and I peeked, and there was my very own handwriting on the paper they were holding! They were cramming in last-minute study time before their test — using my notes from last year! (By then, I don't mind pizza stains anymore. Let them party!)

Finally, Study Night arrives. My study group ranges from four to six girls, besides myself. It's on a first-come-first-serve basis. As soon as a test is announced, I'm bombarded with, "I'm studying with you!" and, "No, *I* am! You did last time!" It feels a little awkward being a king over subjects my age. What am I supposed to do, wave my wand at the girls who asked me first and nod my acceptance of them to my private study group? Maybe I should wait for them to bow in return? Am I supposed to smile or look serious? Which way looks more humble? I'm never sure.

I'm not as full of myself as you think. At this point, I'm more overwhelmed than proud. It almost comes to the point that I have to break up fights.

And anyway, it's not like they want *me*, anyway. They want my brains…and my tolerance and my patience and my grit-your-teeth-before-you-explode-when-you-have-to-explain-yourself-for-the-fourth-time. You know what one of my regulars said once about my Notes *Gemach*? "You know, that must be what you're here for."

Gee, thanks. That's all I'm here for. All I'm worth is some gray matter. If I once don't offer my notes, I don't deserve to be here.

Well, maybe that does have some *hashkafic* basis, but it doesn't exactly feel great to hear it from you.

It's a total given that I will talk blue in the face for an entire five-hour study session. And provide popcorn. And pretzels, if you so order. And a bathroom, and a phone, and paper, and pens, and cold drinks, and sometimes a bed when it gets really late… and a smile.

No, don't worry. It's okay. You're all welcome, all of you. Please do come. I'm glad to help. All I ask is that you understand me.

Understand that I am a human being with choices. And I did choose to help. Please don't treat me as though I owe it to the world. Like, no "please," no "thank you," no "I'm sorry," but only, "Say that again! Penina, you did not explain yourself! You have to be clear!" and, "Tonight you're studying with me. You must. If not, I will fail…"

(But I must say, sometimes it is a real blast. I won't forget the time we studied, about fifteen of us, in the classroom, with pizza, fries, and Cokes — the works — with me at the blackboard. It wasn't bad to play teacher for the day.)

Oh, and another thing to understand: I'm staying up late for you. *Really* late. And you don't always know it, but sometimes I run two study shifts — evening and late-night (up until dawn). No, you don't have to gush your thank you's and get all emotional — I *am* enjoying your company — but please do recognize the facts.

I wish someone would've prepared me and helped me deal with the frustrations and loneliness involved in being the smartest kid in the class. But no, they think I can manage just fine on my own. After I'll, I've got brains.

But you know what? Having brains doesn't mean having everything.

Miri Talks:

The Guidance Counselor

"Confidentiality!"

Miss Gruen prances across the room and cries again, "Confidentiality! Who knows what that means?" Her eyes slowly scan the classroom.

I catch Bracha's eye. She is smirking. Do I know what con-fi-den-shee-al-ity means? No. But who cares? Miss Gruen is weird.

Miss Gruen is a *guidance counselor*. Who needs a *guidance counselor*? Aren't they for kids with *problems*? I don't have *problems*.

Bracha nudges Chani, and Chani laughs, too. Chani coughs to Gila and Chaya, and they giggle along. Soon everyone is snickering.

"Confidentiality means keeping things private. Whatever I discuss privately with anyone will remain private. This is our first and most important rule. We want to respect each other's privacy."

Who will ever speak privately with Miss Gruen?! Please! What are we, problem cases?

As soon as Miss Gruen steps out the door, the class bursts into peals of laughter.

"Confidentiality!" we cry over and over, mimicking Miss Gruen's high-pitched voice.

"Who's first to go to the *guidance counselor*?" Bracha calls out. "Who has a *problem*?"

"Um…I have a problem!" Tova steps forward with a sob. "I don't have any friends." She wipes away an imaginary tear and sniffles. "What should I do, Miss Gruen?"

The class explodes into laughter again.

"You need a friend?" Bracha croons. She puts an arm around Tova's shoulder. "I will be your friend, okay?"

More giggles erupt. Everyone knows Bracha and Tova are best friends.

"Hey — con-fi-den-shee-a-lity!" I sing out. "You can't talk about people's *problems* in public!"

The class doubles over again.

All too soon, though, Miss Gruen is back. But this time Bracha and Tova are no longer friends. No one really knows how it happened, but Tova's joke came true.

And I am stuck in the middle. I was always part of Bracha and Tova's elite group, along with Faigy, Tzipi, and Rochel, and now I have to take sides. Who will I choose? Who will remain my friend?

"What is the definition of a friend?" Miss Gruen asks.

Some girls roll their eyes. Others wink to each other. Finally, Racheli's hand flies up.

"A friend," she announces, "is someone who you like and who likes you. Riiiight?" She looks around the class with a smirk.

"Not true!" Naomi pipes up. "A friend…a friend is someone you can trust."

"And a friend," Chava bellows, "is not a whole group. It's not a *clique*." She spits out the word like it has a horrible taste. She shoots an obvious stare at me and my friends.

"So…so why don't you get a group of friends for yourself? What are you blaming us for?" I yell back. Uh-oh — I regret the words the minute I say them. But the fight is on, and there's almost no stopping.

"Very nice. Veeery nice. Nice of you to talk. You, with all your high-and-mighty friends, huh? Go find yourself your own group. Yeah, right." Chava is on the verge of tears.

I am angry and sympathetic at the same time. I am confused.

No one talks. The tension in the room is thick.

Finally, Miss Gruen speaks. "I see we have a problem here."

One part of me wants to laugh, and the other wants to cry. Chava was always jealous of me and my friends, and it is a problem. But — but Miss Gruen is a *guidance counselor*! I don't need advice from a *guidance counselor*!

I peek at Bracha's face. She is not laughing. She looks sad and confused. If Bracha is not laughing, then no one else is.

"Girls."

Now everyone is listening to Miss Gruen, for once.

"We need to understand what a friend really is. Let me tell you what a friend is *not*, and maybe then you will know what a friend is. A friend is not someone you need to make you popular. A friend is not only a buddy to have fun with. A friend is not only someone to spend time with during recess. So…what is a friend?"

What is a friend, really? No one seems to know. The bell interrupts with a shrill ring.

Bracha jumps up. "Miss Gruen, we'll think about it!" Now, if I know Bracha well enough, I can tell you she is sarcastic.

Miss Gruen seems pleased. "That is a good idea, Bracha."

Bracha smirks ever so subtly.

"We'll review your ideas next time. Class dismissed." Miss Gruen click-clacks out of the classroom.

"What a joke!" Bracha hollers. "Like we need help! Friend, shmiend! We'll figure it out ourselves!"

I peek at Tova. And knowing her, too, I can tell she is about to cry — while everyone else laughs.

But I don't really get the joke. We *do* need to know what true friendship is all about. We need to make amends, and we need to know how.

As soon as I'm home from school, the phone is blasting its war cry. Bracha, Tova, Bracha, Tova. She said this and she said that. Whom should I choose?

Sometimes the battle is fiery, and sometimes it is cold. The insults attack like burning cannonballs, while the air is still frigid and hateful.

I don't want to go to school anymore. I need a friend. I can't take being alone.

At night I cry myself to sleep. I've lost two friends, and I mourn. But what now? How do you make amends? How do you ask for forgiveness? How do you forgive?

I think I need to speak to a guidance counselor. I need guidance here.

I remember Miss Gruen's smile. "Please feel free to come and discuss anything you'd like with me," she'd said.

Yes, there *is* something I'd like to discuss with Miss Gruen. But... will my friends let me feel free to do so?

Aviva Talks:
Hearty and Healthy

The third bout of chest pains and our biology class on heart disease came on the same day.

I'd felt those subtle waves of pain in my chest twice the day before, and now they came again. Right in the middle of biology class on heart disease. I felt my chest contract, then relax, then contract and relax again. And yet again: contract, relax, contract, relax. I clutched my chest and felt the rapid beating of my heart.

I wanted to cry, but I couldn't. I felt frozen, paralyzed. My teacher called it angina pectoris. I had the symptoms of that dreadful heart disease. The horrible, creepy possibility stared me in the face: *I may be sick.*

When the chest pains came for the fourth time while I lay in bed at night, all I wanted to do was huddle under my covers and never come out. I felt safest under my heavy blanket, denying the fears of reality.

Morning came. And with it more chest pains. And I had to get out of bed. I washed my hands slowly, first my right, then my left, and then, hey! My left hand ached terribly. Symptom number two of angina pectoris, here you go. *I'm sick!* I wanted to shout. *Help!*

But I wouldn't dare shout, nor even whisper or even hint about any of it to my parents. I didn't want to worry them. But how on earth was I going to weather this alone? I had no clue. I shuddered. *Where do I go from here?*

I went to school as usual, but I functioned like a zombie. I couldn't listen to a fraction of a lesson, let alone take notes. What was the point anyway? I thought dismally. I was sick and...

Somehow, though, when biology class rolled around, I was alert as ever, hearing the most dire predictions of what was going to happen to my life. Try as I might, I couldn't tune out. I'd never known that would ever be a problem.

I felt so terribly alone. Not only did no one know of my fears, but I was no longer a part of the fun-loving teenager world. My world was a sinister, lonely one. I had a condition. *I was sick.*

When the seventh bout of chest pains came as I lay in bed, wide awake, at three a.m., I burst into tears for the first time since the beginning of the ordeal. It was a nightmare, only I was very much awake. I cried and cried and cried. I was scared. Scared stiff. I was probably very ill and nobody knew about it.

Suddenly, I heard the key turn in the lock of our front door, and then soft footsteps echoed in the silence; I recognized them as my father's walk. My father had just come home now? At three a.m.? That was strange. Oh, I remembered. My father had gone to volunteer at some hospital where a sick, lonely man was undergoing surgery that night.

Hospital. No, no, no! I screamed silently. I clamped my eyes and ears shut — as if that would help anything.

I was suddenly seized with the urge to go and tell my father what was happening. I had to spill the beans; I couldn't take it anymore. I threw on my night robe and dashed out of my room.

"Tatty!" I shouted.

"Aviva!" he whispered loudly, startled.

Oh. It was three o'clock in the morning.

"Tatty," I repeated in a quieter voice, my lower lip quivering.

"What is it?" He looked at me worriedly as he pushed away his plate of grapes on the kitchen table. "Had a bad nightmare?"

I inched closer to the kitchen, falling onto a chair near him.

"Oh, I'm past that." I half-smiled. "Um — well, I really did have a nightmare. While I was wide awake. And it's real." Then it all tumbled out. "Ta, I have terrible chest pains. And my left arm hurts. And that means I'm sick. Tatty, I'm not okay!"

Phew. I'd said it.

My father gave me a strange look. "All right, all right, let's start from the beginning. Why do you think you're sick?" He looked at me intently, scanning my puffy, red eyes.

"My chest hurts. And my left arm hurts. That's" — I lowered my voice to an almost inaudible whisper — "*heart disease.*"

My father smiled. "So we have a practicing doctor on premises. Diagnosing diseases."

"Tatty, listen to me. We learned in school that those two symptoms are a sign of angina pectoris."

"Angina pec — again?"

"Angina pectoris. A form of heart disease. Tatty, I can't take it anymore. I want to check it out!"

I burst into a fresh bout of tears, but this time the tears were freer, less restrained. I wasn't alone in this anymore.

"Aviva, number one, keep calm. Number two, we'll go check it out if you want to."

"Now, Tatty. Please?"

My father threw a glance at the clock. "Looks like I'll be spending the night at the hospital," he quipped.

I threw on my clothes and packed a small bag with a *Tehillim*, some sucking candies, and a book. I prepared for the worst. I shuddered to think of what might be ahead.

My father scrawled a note for my mother and headed to the door, *sefer* in hand. I walked after him, trying to mimic his sure, resolute steps. My father wasn't worried. The thought calmed me. If my father was calm, I could be calm, too.

The tension I'd felt before dissipated as I walked beside my father on the silent streets. I felt so safe and cozy; I didn't even need to ask questions. It was a bit strange, though. Why were we walking and not taking a cab? The local hospital was at least a forty-five-minute walk away! And we were walking in the opposite direction! But my father was leading the way, and so I just followed.

Soon I realized where we were headed. My father was taking me to the Hatzolah garage stationed a short distance from our house. My pulse quickened as my father walked up to the stocky Hatzolah man who was dozing on a chair in the dim garage.

"Ahem…excuse me?" my father said.

"Yes, yes." The man sat up with a jolt and looked at us as he fought back a yawn. "How can I help you?"

"My daughter is complaining of chest pains and pain in her left arm. She's afraid they're symptoms of…a heart problem."

She's afraid, my father had said. *He* didn't seem so in the least.

"Can you check this out?"

There. I was going to be checked out professionally. On one hand, I felt relieved, knowing that a medical professional was taking charge, but at the same time, the magnitude of the moment scared me. It was the moment of truth.

The Hatzolah member called his assistant to take over and asked us to enter his private car.

"I'm taking you to the hospital. The kind of tests your daughter needs to undergo is not in the scope of Hatzolah's work," he explained to my father. "But no need for an ambulance. She could do without that experience." He winked.

We climbed into the car and drove off. I looked out of the window at the black streets whizzing by. Everyone was sleeping soundly, while sleep for me was something I seemed to have done eons ago. I was awake — too awake — living real, real fear.

We arrived at the emergency room, and I was admitted immediately. I was given a bed and told to wait until the doctor would come to see me. My father thanked the Hatzolah man for his kind help, and the man wished us *hatzlachah* and left.

"Aviva, I'm going to check something out at the front desk," my father said. "I'll draw the curtain around your bed, and I want you to try to rest. It's nighttime, you know. Time to dream sweet dreams." He smiled.

I nodded limply. I *was* tired. But try was the most I could do. I knew the jitters inside of me wouldn't allow me one second of rest.

My father drew the green, sickly-looking curtain around my bed. I tried to rest my throbbing head on the pillow, but I was too tense to lie down. I sat cross-legged on my bed and pulled the *Tehillim* out of my bag.

"*Shir hama'alos...*" I started *davening*. It struck me then how little I'd thought of *davening* before. All this time that I'd been feeling chest pains and thinking I was so alone, well, I really *wasn't* alone, just like I'm never alone; I could turn to Hashem at any time.

I began to cry for all I was worth. It felt so cleansing, so comforting, to let out my pain where it really made a difference.

Suddenly, I heard my name. My father was at my bedside, calling my name for what apparently wasn't the first time.

"Aviva, the doctor's here. He'll check you out. But please stay calm; do yourself a favor."

I looked up and saw a tall Japanese man with a white coat that sported the name tag "Dr. Jan Shang."

"Please relax," he said in accented English. "We will be conducting short and painless tests to assess the situation."

He checked my blood pressure and then administered an EKG test to check my heartbeat. On the outside I looked composed; inside, though, I was a wreck.

What if...? Scary thoughts pummeled my brain like hammers. There was a chance that...

The doctor scribbled some things on his clipboard and said he'd review the results and be back in a short while. I wondered what a short while meant, but I didn't ask. I felt too nervous to talk.

I looked at my father. He smiled and opened the *sefer* he'd taken with him. "We're hoping for the best, Aviva, right? And you've been *davening*. That's good." He began learning and became immersed in his own world in seconds.

I fingered my *Tehillim*. I was drained; I didn't feel I had any more strength to *daven*. I put the *Tehillim* in my bag and lay my head against the wall. My mind was racing, and I couldn't stop it. I just wished I could sleep and rest my mind.

I waited...and waited...and waited. That activity, or non-activity, was doing me no good. Just when I felt I would burst, I heard the tapping of shiny shoes. The doctor had returned.

He pulled up a chair near my bed and sat down.

"Mr....Leibowitz?" He looked at my father. My father nodded. "And Aviva?" I looked up and nodded.

"First off, your heart's fine. Totally fine."

I stared at the doctor. "Totally fine? Really?"

"I repeat, ma'am, your heart is absolutely healthy." Here the doctor looked straight at me. "BUT."

But? But? BUT???? Oh, no. My heart began to race.

My father raised his eyebrows, and now I was certain it was true: I was sick, terribly, dreadfully sick.

"Your blood pressure is a tad high," the doctor said.

"So what does that mean?"

Dr. Shang smiled. "Hold it, girl. You're not about to die. Sit back and breathe."

Even I smiled now.

The doctor turned to my father. "Listen, Mr. Leibowitz. Your daughter is in a state of tension. You don't need a psychiatrist to tell you that. Blood pressure shoots up in times of pressure. I do not believe there is any real medical concern here. However, this cannot be proven until she is in a calmer state and we test her blood pressure again.

"My advice? You two go home, get some sleep, and forget you were ever in the hospital. Relax. This is not a dangerous situation. Then, in a couple of days, you can take Aviva for a standard blood pressure test at her pediatrician. I believe that after she calms down, her blood pressure will be completely normal."

My father slowly closed his *sefer* and got up. "Thank you, doctor. We will get going."

I remained motionless on the bed. We were going. But...was I okay or not? How could I relax if I didn't know?

"Come on, Aviva," my father said. "Let's go home."

I finally got to my feet. I was glad to get out of this room full of needles and tears, but I would stay if someone could somehow promise me that I was totally healthy. Then I'd be able to really relax, like everyone was telling me to do. The problem was, it went the other way around: I had to first get out and relax and then do the tests to see if all was really in order or not…

It was five twenty a.m. I walked beside my father, past the endless, noisy cubicles and out into the fresh air. The world was a shade slightly lighter than when we'd come in to the emergency room. That was a good sign.

My father hailed a cab that stood parked near the hospital. We got in silently.

"Aviva, we need to sleep on this," my father said as the car jerked to life and drove off. "I want you to get to bed as soon as we get home, and we'll talk more about it tomorrow, okay?"

"Okay," I said meekly.

When the cab pulled up in front of our house, I had to will my arms to push the door open. They felt like lead. I needed sleep. A lot of it.

We walked into the silent house. The soft lull of my mother's even breathing was music to my ears. At least she was sleeping soundly. One less thing to worry about.

At 5:40 a.m. I fell into bed, and the next thing I knew, it was 2:30 p.m. It was strange to wake up in the middle of everything. I'd missed more than half a day.

I hadn't even *davened*. I suddenly felt the urge to take my siddur and have a long talk with Hashem. Thank goodness for

Minchah. It felt good to so utterly look forward to *davening*. I started slowly, savoring each word of prayer. I had a lot on my mind, and I needed to talk about it. Telling Hashem was the perfect solution.

❋ ❋ ❋

My mother looked at me across the dinner table and sighed. "Aviva, you are so tense. Please relax. You look like a spring that's all wound up."

How did my mother know that that was exactly what I felt like?

My parents exchanged glances, and then my father said, "Aviva, you heard what the doctor said. You are in a state of tension these days, and it's not good. It's making you convince yourself that there's something seriously wrong with you — when really everything is perfectly fine. Except for your stress, that is."

I looked down at my hands. Of course my father was right. Intellectually I knew that. But just knowing that was not helping me calm down.

"Aviva," my father continued, "Mommy and I are going to do our best to get you to relax, but you need to do your part, too. We're going to take you on a two-day vacation, to somewhere nice and green. We're going to have a great time, and you're going to love it — if you allow yourself to. I know it sounds like a contradiction, but we want you to work hard to relax. In practical terms, that means you must force yourself to stop focusing on any aches and pains you may think you have, and instead direct your mind to more positive and pleasant thoughts. Think of the beautiful resort we'll stay at, and all the fun things we'll do together there — Mommy and I are looking forward to this vacation, too! — and you'll see, soon enough you'll calm down."

"And then?" I dared to whisper.

"Then, just like the doctor said, we'll retest your blood pressure, see that everything is fine *b'ezras Hashem*, and we'll put this whole episode behind us!"

I allowed myself a smile as I processed my father's words. A trip. Vacation. No school.

Hey, this didn't sound bad to me!

And, if it meant that I had to put in some effort, like my father said, and work at directing my mind to more positive thoughts... well, I could probably manage to do that, couldn't I?

❈ ❈ ❈

I SAT ON THE GRASS beside my mother, lazily twisting the tall blades around my fingers. This place wasn't only scenic; it was absolutely picturesque. We were at a motel resort in the mountains for two days in the middle of March, enjoying the first brush with spring. The trees were getting greener, the sun brighter, the world a better place. The backdrop was too relaxing to even remember why I was there.

And whenever the unbidden thought did try to worm its way into my mind that maybe there was something seriously wrong with me, and maybe that's why my blood pressure was high, I took a determined stance and steered my mind right back to happy thoughts — like the stunning pool I'd had a dip in that morning...

or the delicious schnitzel sandwiches my father had bought from the kosher takeout store nearby for our supper...or the beautiful scenery that surrounded me wherever I looked... I was surprised at how easy it was, once I really put my mind to it, to "tune out" of scary thoughts and "tune in" to more pleasant ones.

I felt full with a vitality I hadn't known in a long while.

❈ ❈ ❈

THE BLOOD PRESSURE test at the doctor was a cinch.

"Fit as a fox," Dr. Ross declared. My doctor had creative ways of saying everything.

I smiled. My father smiled. Then we laughed.

I was healthy, *baruch Hashem*. My heart was healthy...in every way.

Chavy Talks:
Secrets

A big day was coming up. Big as in BIG, great, exhilarating.

My mother had come to me the night before while I was lying in bed reading a book. I'd made it an early night for a change and treated myself to a good, long read.

My mother walked in as if on tiptoes, very hesitantly. She was coming to tell me something very important, that much was obvious. I shut my book dutifully, sat up in bed, and listened curiously.

"Chavy," my mother began, "I'm going to tell you something because you're one of the older ones in the family, and I know I can trust you." She paused for a moment, looking thoughtful. "I also knew you'd sense something was going on, and I didn't want you to feel left out."

Something was going on.

But what? I couldn't take the suspense.

My mother smiled. "The news is...your big sister Yehudis is soon going to be a *kallah*!"

Wham!

A *kallah*!

I saw white. I heard music. I felt hugs and kisses.

A *kallah*! And not just any *kallah*. We were talking about Yehudis, my favorite big sister, who would soon be a *kallah*!

"When, Mommy?" I whispered with excitement.

"Either tomorrow or the next day."

My stomach flip-flopped.

"Who's...the *chassan*?" The word tasted strange on my tongue.

"Hmmm..."

"Please, Ma, can't I know?"

"The truth is, you don't know the family. The name won't mean anything to you in any case, so I can tell you. His name is Mordechai Handler."

Mordechai and Yehudis. Already they sounded like a great pair.

My mother got up and patted me on the shoulder. "Hope you can still fall asleep," she said with a wink. "And remember, Chavy: this is a secret. The little kids don't know anything, of course."

That meant I was one of the older kids. I was thirteen, a teenager. My mother trusted me.

After my mother left the room, I sure did have a hard time

falling asleep! I felt like dancing, singing, anything but sleeping. I couldn't have asked for better news than this. This wedding would be, for sure, the highlight of the year.

The next day in school, I felt so antsy, I wasn't sure I'd be able to sit through eight straight classes.

Well, finally, the dismissal bell did ring. I grabbed my briefcase, threw on my windbreaker, and practically raced to the classroom door.

"Hey, Chavy!" my best friend Naomi called. "What's the rush?"

Oh. We *did* walk home together every day after school. I'd simply forgotten to wait for her.

"Oh, yeah, Naomi. Sorry. I *am* in a rush, so come along fast, okay?"

"Never knew you could forget to wait for me. You must be in a real rush. What, you have a wedding tonight or something?"

She wasn't so off. I shrugged and laughed.

❋ ❋ ❋

Things were really hectic when I came home. My mother was sliding a batch of cinnamon *rugalach* into the oven; my father was on the phone (on a normal day, he would never even be *home* at this time of day!); Shloimy and Simi were running around the table in a wild race, probably because my mother wasn't on top of them trying to get them to do their homework; and Yehudis was locked up in her room — like she was for the past three days, I suddenly remembered.

"Hi!" I called out.

Nobody seemed to hear me.

"Hi, Mommy!" I came up right near her.

"Oh, hi, Chavy." She looked up and gave me one of her really tired smiles.

"Mommy?"

"Hmmm?" my mother murmured as she rolled out another glob of dough.

"Will it be today?" I stage-whispered.

My mother looked up and put a finger to her lips. "Tomorrow," she mouthed.

I wanted to clap my hands real loud, but I knew I couldn't. Instead I just flashed my brightest smile.

I finally plunked down my briefcase and opened the fridge. "What's there to eat?"

"You can taste a *rugalah*," my mother offered.

"Oooh…" I licked my lips. "I thought you were saving it, so I didn't dare ask."

"Tell me how they are," my mother said.

I peeled a sticky *rugalah* off the baking paper, made a *brachah*, and took a bite. It was absolutely scrumptious. Fit for the occasion.

"They're yum!"

"Good. Now don't fill yourself up on them. We're having supper in an hour."

Just as I was leaving the kitchen, my mother called, "Oh, and Chavy, I made a haircut appointment for you at six at Rina's Salon. Your hair could use a trim. You have to look your best, you know."

"Thanks, Ma. I guess I'll leave after supper."

I dragged my briefcase up the steps to my bedroom. I wanted to get my homework over with first thing.

I started on the math examples, but after two of them, I felt I just didn't have the patience to do any more. I had such an urge to… I didn't even know what.

I took the cordless phone from the base and fingered the buttons. I had to call Naomi.

What were friends for, anyway, if not for sharing secrets? You couldn't keep a secret from a best friend, could you?

Cordless in hand, I headed out of my room and down the steps. I had to find a real private spot to make this phone call. I didn't want anyone discovering this.

I charged down the next flight of stairs to the basement. It made me laugh, but I sat myself in the closet there, shut the door, and only then dialed Naomi's number.

Luckily, Naomi herself picked up.

"Naomi?" I whispered.

"Chavy!" she whispered back. "What's the hush-hush all about?"

"'Kay, I'm going to tell you a secret. A really big secret. Promise you won't tell anyone?"

"Promise."

I drew a deep breath. "Yehudis is getting engaged tomorrow night, Naomi!"

"Wow! I don't believe it! I'm so excited!"

"Okay, Naomi, I can't talk too long. But remember, it's a secret."

"Well, that's what friends are for, right? You can always trust me." Naomi sounded happy.

"Yup, that's what friends are for," I echoed. "Oh, and Naomi?"

"Hmm?"

"I have an appointment for a haircut at Rina's at six o'clock tonight. Wanna meet me there?"

"Sure thing."

"See you then!"

I finally opened the closet door and inhaled the freedom. Phew, finally some fresh air.

I leaped up the steps two by two and ran straight to my room. Now I really had to finish my homework fast. I still had a full agenda for the evening.

✸ ✸ ✸

Rina's Salon was a great, cozy place to be. There were plush couches just waiting for you to sink into while you waited for your turn. Happy music was always playing, and best of all was plump, bubbly Rina, who fussed over you until you looked just right.

Naomi and I sat schmoozing on the leather sofa as Rina was finishing up with another customer, who happened to be a girl from my school.

As usual, Rina was prattling away, and she soon began firing questions in our direction.

"So how are you, girls? Who's the lucky one today? Any special occasion coming up?"

"Today it's Chavy's turn," Naomi spoke for me. "She's the one with the occasion."

Gulp. I couldn't believe what I was hearing. But before I could stop her, Naomi was prattling on.

"A sister's engagement is a special one, isn't it?"

What in the world was she doing?

As soon as the words left her mouth, I saw her face blush a deep crimson. She snuck a glance at me, and our eyes met. She looked stricken, fear filling her features, as if she'd just met up with a lion.

She had clearly made a mistake. The words had just slipped out. It was too late, though; Rina and the customer she was working on, an eighth grader in our school, had heard. There was no taking that back.

Rina was smart enough to notice that it was a mistake and went on chattering about other things as though nothing had happened. Bless Rina.

A half hour later, Naomi and I left the buzzing salon in silence. She didn't want to bring up THE topic, and neither did I, so we left it at that.

❋ ❋ ❋

BEFORE I WENT TO SLEEP that night, I thought of Mirel. Mirel was my second-to-best friend. She'd be really insulted if she found out that I only told the news to Naomi and not her. I had to tell her, I really did.

I headed for the same private spot again; it was safest there.

I dialed Mirel's number and felt beads of perspiration on my forehead and neck as I waited for someone to pick up. When I was just about to hang up, Mirel's little brother finally answered the phone.

By the time Mirel came to the phone, I was totally drenched in sweat. The smell of musty notebooks was getting to me, and I couldn't wait to get out of my hiding spot.

"Mirel?" I whispered.

"Who is this?"

"Mirel, fast. It's Chavy. Look, I'm telling you a really big secret and you have to promise not to tell anyone."

"Okay," she drawled.

"Mirel, Yehudis is getting engaged tomorrow!"

"Wow, I'm so excited for you! I know what it's like; when Elchanan got engaged, it was the best day of my life."

"But please, don't tell anyone, okay?"

"Of course I won't. But who's the *chassan*?"

I bit my lip. Well, the truth was, she probably didn't know the family anyway. The name wouldn't mean anything to her; it couldn't hurt to tell it to her.

I lowered my voice to a barely audible whisper. "Mordechai Handler."

The closet door was flung open.

My sister Yehudis stood there, glaring at me.

Yikes!!!

"Get off the phone," she said evenly.

"Uh, Mirel," my voice shook so hard I could hardly get the words out, "I-I have to go."

I punched the off button with a clammy finger and let the phone fall from my hands.

Yehudis didn't move an inch. She just stood looking at me, hands folded across her chest.

I felt as stupid as a flopped actress in a play.

My hair was totally wet from sweat by now. I probably looked like a wreck, and I felt even worse. I just wanted to disappear.

Yehudis didn't say a word. She just gave me another glare and then stalked out of the room and up the stairs.

I plopped back down on the floor, right there in the closet. I hugged my knees to my chin and buried my face in my lap.

That was what I'd call "The Most Horrific Moment in My Life."

I put the incident out of my mind, though, as I lay in bed later that night, and focused instead on the upcoming engagement. There was so much to think about, and I felt heady with the excitement.

❋ ❋ ❋

Something was just not right.

It was quiet at home, too quiet.

My mother was sitting at the kitchen table, sighing to some unknown person on the phone.

"We'll just have to learn to live with it," she was saying. "These things happen."

What things happen?

My mother had written a note for the secretary the night before, asking her to allow me to leave school at three o'clock. The engagement was supposed to be that evening.

But here I was, still panting from having raced all the way home, expecting to see a whirlwind of activity in the house — but instead being met by a kind of foreboding stillness.

Where was Yehudis? Why was she not prancing before the mirror, fixing her hair and putting on her jewelry?

And why was my mother not dressed already?

And the table — why, the *chassan's* family was expected soon, and it was nearly bare — that is, except for some random papers!

What in the world was going on?

Finally, my mother put down the phone and, with a very loud sigh, propelled herself up from the chair like she was under a ton of bricks.

"M-Mommy?"

"Hmm?" My mother reached for the kettle and filled it with water. She was making herself a coffee. That wasn't a good sign. A second coffee in one day was reserved for highly stressful, tiring days.

"When...are they coming?"

"Who?"

Who? Did my mother really not know who I was talking about?

"Oh..." My mother laughed — was it bitterly? "I was just a bit absentminded." Scooping a spoonful of coffee into her cup, she said slowly, "Chava'le, things are not going exactly as planned."

Okay. Fair enough. "So it'll be tomorrow instead?" I asked hopefully. I had the queasy feeling that things weren't as simple as that, but the oblivion was good for the moment.

"Um...probably not."

"So —"

"It...may not happen, Chavy."

My stomach dropped to my knees. *This can't be happening.*

It was just…over?

"Why, Mommy?"

A shadow passed over my mother's face. I realized it hadn't been the right question at the right moment.

"Chavy."

I was old enough, I guess, to realize that I wasn't old enough to know the answers.

"I'm sorry, Mommy," I whispered.

I left the kitchen, the silence between us being too awkward to bear. I dragged myself up the steps to my bedroom, closed the door behind me, and fell onto my bed in a daze.

It was like a play had started, an awesome, dazzling drama, and then it had suddenly come to a halt. The music stopped, the curtains were down, the lights were out.

And there was an audience, too. My heart skipped a beat. I had to inform the audience, "Sorry, everybody, but you'll have to go home. The entertainment's over."

❋ ❋ ❋

IT WAS AN ADULTS-ONLY DINNER that night, in which I, proudly enough, was allowed to participate. The two little ones were put to bed earlier than usual.

There was mostly silence during dinner, except for my father's intermittent jokes he was evidently trying very hard to come up with to lighten the atmosphere. Yehudis and I didn't exchange even the tiniest glance.

It was as we were clearing off the table that my mother said, "You know, I'm so glad the whole story remained between us and isn't out on the streets. Yehudis and all of us can feel comfortable going out and meeting people without feeling everyone's eyes on our backs. Right, Abba?"

"Yes," my father heartily agreed. "That's what family's all about — privacy, trust, and security."

That was when Yehudis gave me THE LOOK. It was a mixture of pain, hurt, and disappointment, and it didn't make me feel any good.

And it got me thinking about what friends, and family, are really all about.

Itty Talks:
Backstage

I watch my classmates fidget in their seats. I squirm, too.

Who will be Director's Assistant, Dance Head, Main Actress? Which girls will get the top play jobs? Only Mrs. Schonberg knows the answers — and she is about to tell us.

I know I will get one of the good jobs — I just wonder which. I'd always starred in plays, choirs, carnival preparation, you name it. It's not a secret that I have a lot of talent.

Mrs. Schonberg begins: "Tova Adler — Director's Assistant!"

A round of applause. I signal a thumbs-up to Tova. Good for you, Tova!

It was only natural that Tova would be Director's Assistant. And it's also only natural that I'll be one of the next names on the list.

But I'm not Dance Head, Main Actress, or Choir Head. I'm not even in charge of costumes or props.

I get the honorary title of — get the balloons and streamers — Backstage Helper!

Backstage. I get to be backstage from the beginning of the play's creation until its celebrated finale. I will prepare the actresses' costumes so they can change quickly between scenes, and then fold and put away the costumes from the previous scenes. I will schlep tables, benches, and couches on and off the stage between scenes. I will be dressed all in black, so no one mistakenly sees me from the audience — though the stage curtains will be drawn anyway. I will work quickly and discreetly, so no one realizes anything's being done at all.

"And that takes real talent," Mrs. Schonberg notes with a dramatic nod.

Talent. Right now I need a hefty dose of talent not to cry. I need to be a real good actress for that. That's the talent I need.

Play practice devours every hour of the school day — whether the teachers like it or not. Even when we're learning Chumash, or history, or science, production hums in the background. Girls are called in and out of class. The dance heads need their dance approved by the principal, the sewing heads need to go out and buy material when the stores are still open, the choir heads need to run solo tryouts. But I sit through history, science, and math. I announce that I'm available to lend my notes to whoever missed class, because I didn't. I'm only in charge of backstage, after all — sorry, that should be Backstage. I only need to be at the actual complete rehearsals, which are always after school hours.

At rehearsals I hear (I can't see from backstage) the beautiful choir songs. I can just imagine my best friend, Chanie, orchestrating the choir from in front of the stage, nodding encouragingly to the shy singer, motioning to the soloist to start, prodding the harmonists to sing a little louder. She confers with the pianist and the play director, asking them both for feedback and suggestions.

In the next scene, Tzivie, the main actress, delivers a heartrending monologue, breaking down in tears in the middle. Her voice cracks as she speaks, betraying an admirable depth of emotion. After the scene, she drops onto a chair, covered in sweat. She has worked hard, but it's all worth it. She knows just how to bring tears to people's eyes.

The dancers come backstage with sweaty costumes, too (which I have the privilege to handle). They have twirled and danced and jumped and made the audience gasp in admiration.

And I could have done all that. I can sing, I can act, and I can dance. I can enrapture an audience, and I can pull at people's heartstrings.

But I am a backstage helper — oops, that should be with a capital B. And it takes real talent not to be noticed — as Mrs. Schonberg says.

I am bitter and sad and jealous, but I know it's not getting me anywhere. I will do the same job whether I sulk or I smile. And it's no fun to sulk. I may not enjoy using my talents in this play, but I could have fun. This is one choice I do have.

Backstage helpers have the advantage of being — well, backstage. They see the actresses tremble before the scene, and then come back exhilarated. They see the soloists bite their lips before the choir, and then come back all smiles.

After so many rounds of rehearsal, I get used to being Adviser, Encourager, and Last-Minute Hair Brusher. I make friends with girls I'd never even seen before in school — and wouldn't have seen if I wasn't backstage — as I watch the mass goings and comings onstage and offstage.

I worry and hope for the actresses when they walk onto stage, and feel proud of them when they come back. I'm not the actress myself, but I feel for every one of them as if I were them.

I don't have to be the Main Actress, or any actress, to feel, or smile, or encourage. I don't have to star in the play to be me.

My role in the play is not me. I can be me whether I'm onstage or backstage.

And that's the best role of all.

Leah'le Talks:
Sink or Swim

The grass in my sister's camp pictures looks so green and the wooden cabins more rustic than I'd ever seen. I smile sadly. "I wish I can go, too."

Bracha turns to me sharply. "So why didn't you ever say so? You've been insisting for the past who-knows-how-many years that you only want to work in the city day camp in the summer. Maybe Mommy can still register you in camp, if you want to go."

Well, I do want to go to that green place with the wooden cabins in the picture… I am a bit of a stick-in-the-mud homebody, but I really should get over it. Those serene pictures look so inviting…

I am already a high school girl. I should go to camp. I must go to camp like everyone else.

That's it. I'm going. I hope it isn't too late to register.

My mother is glad, just like I thought she'd be, and she uses some connections to get me a quick acceptance letter for the first half of camp.

✽ ✽ ✽

I clutch the list of "Things to Bring to Camp" and read it again. Shirts, skirts, sneakers, sunglasses, cap, suntan lotion...

Bracha and I pile up on colorful beach towels, goggles, bathing caps, and suntan lotion. We get swimming slippers, bathrobes, and flashlights.

But the fun is only starting. We make a trip to the supermarket and load up on nosh, nosh, and more nosh. We've got to fill up for a whole month. We empty the shelves of sour sticks, potato chips, and peanut chews. Finally, we push our overflowing shopping cart to the cash register, much to the amusement of the cashier.

"You making a party or somethin'?" she drawls as she scans the tenth pack of wafers.

"No, we're going to camp."

"Oh, camp! Lucky girls. I wish I'd gone to camp. Have fun!"

I'm sure I will.

✽ ✽ ✽

I do have fun. On the first day, at least. The counselor is friendly, the girls look nice, and the campgrounds really are beautiful. The theme song is set to a catchy tune, and it plays over and over in my head the whole day.

But that night, as I lie in bed listening to the sound of the crickets, I find that I cannot fall asleep. I am in camp, near the woods, in a bunk with a bunch of unfamiliar girls. I will jump rope, play ball, and go swimming in the pool every day. Ouch. I don't want any of that. I'm no sports girl, and I'm terrified of water.

Ouch! I clutch my stomach. I turn to the right side, and then the left, then lie on my stomach, then on my back. I sit up and lie back down. I count sheep. Ouch again. Cramps rip across my stomach. I will never fall asleep this way. But I cannot lie in bed anymore. I cannot lie here awake — and alone. I have to get out. I throw on a robe and socks and walk out to the bunkhouse porch.

I look around the empty campgrounds, and a tear rolls down my cheek. Ouch. The cramps attack me again. But my thoughts are even more painful: I might never fall asleep tonight, and I'll have to battle my stomachaches here in the silent night, all by myself...

It's lonely in bed, but it's lonely out here, too. More tears jump to my eyes.

"What's the matter?"

I jump back. I hadn't noticed anyone coming. Shaindel, my counselor, puts her hand on my shoulder.

"Leah'le, what's the matter?"

"I...my stomach really hurts and...and I can't sleep."

My counselor takes my hand. "The camp nurse here keeps really late hours," she says. "Let's go to the infirmary and have you checked out."

❋ ❋ ❋

"Stomach cramps? Hmmm. Did you eat too much junk today?" Mrs. Abramovitz, the camp nurse, asks with a smile in her eyes.

"No." My huge nosh carton is still sealed.

"Okay, so I'll give you a hot water bottle and you'll sleep here tonight. Let's hope you'll feel better tomorrow morning."

Mrs. Abramovitz shows me into a small room and points to a bed covered with a bright pink and yellow bedspread. "Feel right at home, Leah'le."

Tears fill my eyes again and I blink, trying to push them back. I feel at home, I feel safe, I feel happy…and that's why I am crying. Mrs. Abramovitz's place is so different from the silent and lonely bunkhouse I've just been in.

The phone rings. A plate of homemade cake sits in the center of the kitchen table. A sagging bookshelf hangs opposite the bed that I am shown.

Home. The sounds and smells and sights of a real home.

I take the hot water bottle from Mrs. Abramovitz, but I'm not sure my stomach hurts anymore.

"Feel free to use the shower — it's there down the hall — and take anything you want — from the fridge, from the bookshelves — anything. Make yourself right at home."

The shower room smells fresh and inviting. I didn't take a shower yet that night (confession!), because the lines for it were so long. I'm happy to take a hot and calming shower right now, with no one banging impatiently on the door.

After my shower, I choose a book from the shelf and fall onto the soft bed. The book's from my favorite series, and I'm glad to see the rest of the series there, too, so I could read tomorrow…and the next day… Hey, I might feel better by then, and I won't be in the infirmary anymore. I frown. Odd as it sounds, I kind of don't want to feel better…

But of course, that's just what happens. By morning, my stomach cramps are gone. And Mrs. Abramovitz's freshly fried omelet and perfectly-cubed salad fill me with delicious satisfaction — hardly what I'd felt after the greasy spaghetti and meatballs dinner I'd eaten last night in the huge, noisy dining room.

Mrs. Abramovitz speaks softly into the phone, rocking on the recliner. A fresh batch of chocolate cookies emits a heavenly aroma from the oven.

I step out onto the balcony and watch a group of girls kicking a soccer ball in the field. Cries of triumph and disappointment travel up to me. They are playing, and I am not. They are running, and I am not. And I'm happiest this way. Sports were never my thing.

I *daven* slowly, dreading Mrs. Abramovitz's inevitable question. I won't lie. I feel better, but…but…I want to stay.

In the infirmary?! I could imagine Mrs. Abramovitz exclaiming.

In the infirmary?! she'd ask again, her eyes opening wide when I'd nod my head.

Yes, in the infirmary. In a place with safe adults and the smell of fresh food. With a bed with pink and yellow bedspread. Where I don't have to try to be popular and flop at Machanayim.

But I am out of the infirmary by ten a.m., so I can "run and catch up with the other girls at the pool." I swallow the lump in my throat. *No thanks.*

My bunkmates are racing across the length of the pool. The deep end is ten feet deep. Oh, no. I can't get anywhere close to that part. I like the baby part of the pool — that is, if you forced me to get into the water at all. If you didn't, I'd be happy to tan in the sun with another book from the twenty-part series in Mrs. Abramovitz's infirmary.

But I get into the water and even risk the four-and-a-half-feet-deep section. After all, I have come to camp to have fun and make friends. I have to try. No one will be able to say I didn't.

Now my bunkmates are in a circle, playing The Birthday Game. Everyone chants the names of the months, and you dunk into the water at the month of your birthday. From across the circle, Fraidy shouts, "So you're feeling better, Leah'le?"

I laugh. "Oh, totally. Just a little stomachache."

They're up to March. My birthday is in September, and in just half a minute, I'll have to dunk in the water. I can't dunk — I'm terrified of being underwater. Uh-oh — here come the cramps again. *No, I'm not okay! My stomachache is back!*

September! I don't dunk. Instead I laugh with everyone when Miri's bathing cap floats away and she swims frantically to retrieve it.

December!

"Hey, you don't have a birthday?" the girl at my right (name still unknown) asks.

"Um…hey, I guess I forgot!" I try to laugh, but I can't. My stomach is clenching in knots.

"Let's race again, 'kay?" a tall, lanky girl, who looks like she can get across the pool in half the strokes of everyone else, calls out.

I'm cold. I'm shivering. I want to get out. I don't want to race anyone anywhere. I want to get out!

I have to get out, and I will. I don't care if anyone whispers behind my back. I just have to get out.

❉ ❉ ❉

I AM BACK on the pink and yellow bed, reading the second book in the series. Mrs. Abramovitz is worried. Is it the camp food that's bothering my stomach? Is it a virus?

By morning, of course, my cramps have disappeared. "Hopefully for good this time, so you can enjoy camp," Mrs. Abramovitz says.

Secretly, I hope not.

❉ ❉ ❉

BUT I KEEP TRYING and trying, doing my best to enjoy camp, and, surprise of surprises, I do end up liking camp! Well, some of it. I like the *kumzitz* at night and the amazing *shiur* in the morning. I like sitting on the grass and schmoozing during rest hour, and I like noshing in the bunkhouse with camp friends on Shabbos afternoon. And I love getting my parents' letters from home and writing letters back to them.

But I hate playing soccer, or Machanayim, or kickball. I couldn't throw a ball right if you coached me the whole summer. I am still scared to swim, and I don't like cheering at the top of my lungs.

I hate the major trip to the water park and the night hike in the woods.

I guess you can say I'm not the coolest kid in the bunk. Still, I make some friends and we enjoy spending time together.

Now there's only fifteen days left of camp, and then I'm home. Oh, to be back home again — in my real home, this time, not just a homey camp infirmary... I can't wait!

I know I'm an exception, but, I'm discovering — that's okay. I suppose I'm just not a "camp kid," but you know what? I can be a great kid anyway.

Nechami Talks:
Mistake!

How do you write *rational* with a spelling mistake? *Racional*, right? That's a sensible mistake.

So here I go — I carefully write *racional* on my spelling test.

I look at *racional* again, and then once more, before handing in my test. Good, I have a mistake on my paper. Now I can hand it in.

Now I will get a 95% on my test. For the first time!

I walk up nonchalantly to hand in my test. I hesitate for only a second before I place it on the teacher's desk, and then firmly add it to the pile of tests. There. No taking it back. My mistake is on my paper for good. Now I can complain like everyone else, "Well, what does she expect! The test was so hard!"

I will get my test back and have what to talk about with everyone else. I will clap my hand over my mouth and moan, "Oh, no! I got *rational* wrong! What a mistake!" Then I'll compare my paper with the other girls and find my mistake. "Oh, I wrote c instead of t! That is so silly of me! How could I forget?"

But the next day, I regret my actions. Why should I only get a 95%? Why should I, if I can get a 100%?

Maybe I can still fix it.

"Mrs. Blum?"

"Yes?"

"Can I, um, fix a mistake on my test, that I, uh, really knew was a mistake?"

"You knew you were writing the wrong answer?"

"Um…yes."

Mrs. Blum looks at me strangely. "No, once you hand it in, it's in. I'm sorry."

I am also sorry. My grades won't be a smooth list of 100% anymore. I'll have a 95% messing it up in the middle. My very first 95%.

But I wanted to be like everyone else. And I got what I wanted.

Miriam Talks:
My Choice

The oatmeal cookie dangled between my thumb and pointer. I hoped Mrs. Brody wasn't about to offer me another one.

"Did you drink a hot cocoa yet?"

"No, but it's really okay, Mrs. Brody. I-I'm not really thirsty, and I'm also in a rush to get to school." She ignored me, filling the kettle with water. I drew a deep breath. "Really, thanks, Mrs. Brody. I don't want to be late to school."

She eyed me sharply. "It's not too late. You need a hot drink. I won't let you go like that. Come here and sit down. I'll make you one."

Oh, no. Double oh, no. If it wasn't bad enough that I had to drink a hot cocoa in Mrs. Brody's house — *she was making it*, on top of that!

I wouldn't know if the cup and spoon she'd use were clean, and I wouldn't be able to smell the milk first.

I sat down on a black plastic stool — one of Mrs. Brody's two kitchen chairs — and sighed. There was just no way to get out of this. There was no leaving Mrs. Brody without drinking her hot cocoa and stale oatmeal cookies.

Mrs. Brody hobbled to the table, balancing a brown mug, which she placed on the table in front of me. "Drink," she ordered.

I searched for a clean spot so I could put down the oatmeal cookie. I sifted through the pile of crumpled napkins on the table until I found a clean one, and placed the cookie on it.

I took tiny, forced sips as I watched Mrs. Brody rummage in her fridge for something to eat. She finally took out a container of tuna fish spread and sat down next to me. She opened the container and spooned some tuna out with a cracker.

"Sho, what time are you coming tonight?" she asked me with a full mouth as some tuna shot out at my chin. I feared I would vomit.

"Ummm…I guess at nine," I finally mumbled.

That night, I was back at nine, with my bag of clothing and schoolbooks. After helping Mrs. Brody hang up some washed robes and socks on the laundry line outside, and finishing my math homework, I finally lay down on the brown sofa to sleep. Struggling for a comfortable position on the narrow, prickly couch, I thought of my sister's birthday party that I'd just missed. My mother had made a special cream cake for the occasion, and my sisters and I had designed a huge birthday card in the shape of a nine and signed it. Everyone back home was having a merry time...while I was left to hang an old lady's fraying robes and socks on the laundry line.

It was the third night I was sleeping at Mrs. Brody's that week. Thankfully, the next day was Shabbos and I'd be spared. At least for Shabbos, Mrs. Brody had a regular volunteer.

I wished my parents would've forbidden me to sleep at Mrs. Brody's. But they didn't, and I couldn't say no. I didn't want to turn down a mitzvah!

So sleep at Mrs. Brody's I did — if you could call it sleep. I'd doze off, only to be awakened twenty minutes later by Mrs. Brody's loud snoring. Then I'd fall asleep again, and an hour later I'd be up with Mrs. Brody's loud groans: "Miriam! Please open the light! I can't see the way to the bathroom!" Then I'd spend another twenty minutes waiting for Mrs. Brody and helping her back to bed.

In the morning, I'd feel anything but refreshed. I'd slap cold water on my face, brush my teeth, and comb my hair, and hope nobody would notice the dark circles under my eyes. And the morning wasn't the end of my troubles. Morning always brought the ubiquitous hot cocoa and stale oatmeal cookies that I had to somehow deal with.

In school I found myself dreaming up excuses to get out of sleeping at Mrs. Brody's. Once it was a sprained ankle, or else I had to help my mother, or I had a first cousin's wedding.

But I wouldn't lie, and none of these things seemed to be happening. My ankle remained intact, my mother had another three capable daughters to help her, and none of my cousins were even engaged.

When Mrs. Brody called, she immediately had me in her net. The conversation always started with: "Miriam, what time are you coming?" Never, "*Are* you coming?" or, "*Can* you come?"

But...if she was expecting me to come, then I couldn't turn her down. And so I'd take a shower, pack my things, and trudge the five long blocks to Mrs. Brody's house.

Mrs. Brody was an old, poor widow whose only child, a son, lived overseas. My family had been helping her out ever since we were her neighbors, and continued caring for her even after we moved away. For some reason, I was always stuck with the unlucky task of sleeping at Mrs. Brody's.

It was so lonely at Mrs. Brody's house. I wished I could bring a friend to sleep with me there, but there was no extra bed — not that you could call the brown sofa I slept on, a bed. I'd fallen off that narrow couch more than once. In the middle of the night, I'd suddenly find myself on the floor as my shoulder jabbed into a nearby chair. It would take me a minute or two before I could even try getting myself up, and then there were the dust balls all over my nightgown. Ouch. Ugh.

Purim was soon around the corner. I prepared a special *mishloach manos* package for Mrs. Brody, putting in the things I knew an old lady would appreciate: grape juice, prune hamantaschen, and some cut-up fresh fruit. I walked over to Mrs. Brody's house on Purim afternoon, on the way to the *seudah* at my aunt's house. It was my job, of course; my sisters kept their distance, too afraid to get involved with Mrs. Brody. I, ever the goody-goody, was unofficially in charge of the "case."

I walked into Mrs. Brody's apartment building and climbed the three flights to her apartment. I knocked, and she opened the door immediately. The house was eerily quiet, in stark contrast to the singing and dancing on the streets outside. Poor woman. Purim was probably not very different from any other day for her.

"Good, you're early today!" Mrs. Brody said as I placed my package on the kitchen table.

"Early?" I could guess what was coming, and my heart sank.

"Yes, you came to sleep here early — what is it now, five thirty? — instead of waiting till nine at night!"

"Er...Mrs. Brody, um...it's Purim, and..."

"Yeah, yeah. I know it's Purim. My ears are busting from all the noise outside."

"...And I...have a *seudah* at my aunt's house..."

"Oh? The Purim *seudah*, aha. Oh, well, so you'll come afterward."

Afterward? *Afterward?!*

Our family Purim *seudos* always stretched late into the night. Most years we finished close to midnight!

"Mrs. Brody..." No, I couldn't say it. I couldn't tell her that our family *seudah* lasted until midnight when the woman didn't have any family to eat with at all.

"Um...okay, I'll come."

There goes my night again! And on Purim, no less! I fumed after the words left my mouth. I was stuck sleeping at Mrs. Brody's — *yet again* — and would be missing the best hours of our family Purim *seudah*. All my cousins were going to be there. The big *seudah* had become a family tradition, with Aunt Faiga hosting my grandparents and their six children with their families every Purim. Some of the uncles got drunk, and there was lots of singing, dancing, and of course loads and loads of nosh.

It was so typical. I always ended up missing all the fun stuff.

My family was already at Aunt Faiga's when I came. My mother, balancing a heaping platter of potato blintzes, met my eyes and smiled.

"Good for you, Miriam. You did a big mitzvah. I'm proud of you."

I forced a smile. My mother was proud of me. Let her be. I wasn't proud of myself one bit; I wished I could muster the courage to turn down Mrs. Brody's request.

My worries were momentarily forgotten when my boisterous cousins, a family of six boys under the age of nine, bounded in through Aunt Faiga's door.

"*A freilichen Purim! A freilichen Purim!*"

One of the boys turned up the music volume, and they started dancing.

I looked at my watch. It was already six thirty. A heavy dread clutched me, making me feel dizzy for a moment. In two and a half hours I'd have to leave this fun to sleep at Mrs. Brody's.

As I stood ladling steaming soup into bowls in the kitchen, I mumbled to my mother that I'd promised Mrs. Brody that I'd sleep at her house that night. My mother gave me a long, thoughtful look. "Miriam, it's unbelievable what you're ready to give up on for this mitzvah. The fact that it's hard for you makes it so much more precious."

Tell me no, Mommy! Tell me you don't want me to miss the highlight of the year! Tell me you forbid me to stretch myself that far! Tell me you need me here! Tell me...

But my mother wasn't telling me anything. She was already in the dining room, serving the hot bowls of soup and laughing at the sight of six-year-old Dovy's amateur attempts to act like a policeman.

Nice try, I thought to myself wryly. I had hoped my mother might finally dissuade me from going to Mrs. Brody, but instead, she just encouraged me.

Though I sat at the *seudah* table, my mind was a million miles away. I couldn't even focus on Uncle Simcha's jokes. I kept tuning in and out, looking at the clock, then at my watch, and trying to figure out which gave me an extra minute to stay.

Eight forty-five. Fifteen minutes to go. We were only up to the main course. Great, I'd have to miss dessert. Aunt Faiga had made a scrumptious chocolate fudge ice cream sandwiched in a delicious crunch. She had even let me have a peek when I'd come. Now I wouldn't even get to taste it. I was too embarrassed to ask for a portion before everyone else. I'd do without the ice cream — I'd have Mrs. Brody's stale cookies instead. Yippee!

Nine o'clock. I got to my feet and went to the kitchen to thank Aunt Faiga.

"Um, Aunt Faiga…"

"Oh, Miriam, good you're here," she said distractedly as she tried to steady the tipping stack of dishes in the sink. "I'll need help cutting up the apple pie and arranging it on a platter."

"Oh. Um, sorry, Aunt Faiga, um…I was actually going to tell you that I have to leave now, so I wanted to thank you."

Aunt Faiga turned to look at me in surprise. "You're going?"

I nodded.

"May I ask where you're going that's more important than our annual family Purim *seudah*?"

"I promised Mrs. Brody — remember her? — that I would sleep at her house, and —"

"You're going to sleep at Mrs. Brody's *tonight*? Miriam, I didn't know there's a hidden *tzaddekes* in my very own kitchen!"

She started for the dining room, holding a platter of cookies and motioning for me to follow.

The dining room was unusually quiet. Uncle Shimshi was talking. He always got drunk on Purim. I knew this would be interesting. His eyes shut tightly, he was swaying wildly, saying, "So Purim is a time of *simchah*, and what is *simchah*?" His voice took on the Gemara singsong. "True *simchah* is *simchah shel mitzvah*. Aha! *Azoi*?" He banged his fist on the table. "Is our happiness today a result of mitzvos? If it is not, it is not true *simchah*. So we must remember," he sang out, "to channel our *simchah* to gratitude to Hashem for the *nes* of Purim, and not because we like wine! Or steak!" He threw up his plate of meat a little too wildly, and his half-eaten portion of meat fell onto ten-year-old Yitzy's yarmulke. Everyone burst out laughing, but Uncle Shimshi was totally oblivious. "Or stuffed cabbage!" he shouted, sticking his fork into a piece of stuffed cabbage from the center platter and dangling it in the air. "Or Coke!" He picked up the Coca-Cola bottle that was in front of him and banged it back down on the table, toppling some cups around it.

Then he grew serious. "So you see, *rabboisai*, *simchah* is only true when it comes from a mitzvah, and a mitzvah is only real if it comes with *simchah*!"

He stopped short and looked at his plate. "And who stole my grilled, mushroom-cream-smothered steak?" He glared at the men and kids around the table. Everyone burst out laughing again.

Nine ten. I was late already.

I'd have to make my goodbyes quick now. I waved hastily, smiling to my grandmother and mother, and turned to leave.

I opened the front door, and a blast of cold air hit me in the face. I started feeling an almost uncontainable lump form in my throat. I had to hurry and get out. I didn't want anyone to catch me crying.

"Hey, who's leaving?" Uncle Shimshi boomed just before the door closed behind me. "I'm in the middle of my *drashah*! Who's got such guts to leave in the middle of Shimshi's *drashah*?!"

I turned around and peeked inside the house.

"Miriam! What's up, Miriam? Why so early? Purim is only once a year!"

I said nothing.

"And why the long face?" he challenged. "It's Purim today! Ha, ha, ha, ha, ha!"

I couldn't help but chuckle.

Then my mother spoke up. "She's on the way to do a mitzvah, Uncle Shimshi. Let her go."

No! No! No! No!

"To do a mitzvah, aha! So why are you so sad? *A mitzvah tit men b'simchah!* Did you not hear my *drushah*, Miriam?" he asked, mimicking a Hungarian accent. "You weren't listening, eh?"

If I wasn't choking back tears, I would have found this hysterically funny. Uncle Shimshi was a quiet, unassuming man. The alcohol was really having an effect on him.

"Come in and close the door, Miriam. Tell us which mitzvah you are going to do."

"I…I'm going to sleep at an old lady's house."

"Aha. Very nice. But you're not happy about it. So don't go."

Huh?

"You're forcing yourself to go even though you don't want to, right?"

I nodded.

"It's a mitzvah only if you choose to do it and you're happy about it. That's not something I made up; Rav Dessler says that. If you can't first teach yourself to say no, and when you say yes, it is really honest, then there's no point in doing the *chessed*."

I kept my eyes on Uncle Shimshi, not knowing what to do. Suddenly, he burst into a lively round of "*Ivdu Es Hashem B'simchah*," and all the men joined him.

I was still rooted to my spot, the door weighing on my side.

I met my mother's eyes. She got up from her seat and walked into the kitchen, and I followed her. Aunt Faiga was already cutting squares of chocolate fudge ice cream and arranging them on plates.

"So, Miriam, you're staying, right?" Aunt Faiga asked as she handed me plates of ice cream to serve.

"Miriam, you really weren't happy about it?" my mother said in an almost-whisper.

I nodded. I already felt tears welling up in my eyes.

Aunt Faiga looked at me and took the plates from my hands. "You go sit down, Miriam. You need some time to get over this."

I sat down heavily on a kitchen chair. Aunt Faiga walked over to me and sat down on another chair beside me.

"Miriam," Aunt Faiga said, putting her arm on my shoulder. "You don't have to feel bad about this. If you don't feel up to willingly choosing to sleep at Mrs. Brody's, then it is not for you. There's no point in forcing yourself to do this *chessed*. You heard what Uncle Shimshi said. And don't worry, he knows what he's saying. When you're high from too much alcohol, you say the real, inner truth."

Now I couldn't hold the tears back anymore. I started crying, and I cried and cried. It felt good. But when the kids started peeking in to the kitchen to watch me, I escaped to the privacy of the bathroom. I cried for twenty whole minutes. With the tears, I let out my pent-up stress and frustration, and finally, relief. When I calmed down, I felt tired, but happy. I wasn't going to force myself into doing anything.

I washed my face with cold water and went back to the kitchen.

Aunt Faiga was there again, this time arranging roasted almonds and cashews in a sectional candy dish.

"Now the real fun begins," Aunt Faiga said with a wink.

I smiled. I was more than ready for fun. But I had to do something first.

I placed a call to an organization that pairs volunteers with people in need, and asked the woman who answered the phone if she might be able to find a volunteer on such short notice. I had always known about the organization, but had forced myself not to give away the mitzvah. Now I knew that I could — and should — share the mitzvah when I needed to.

The woman sounded astonished; she told me I wouldn't believe it, but just a few minutes earlier, a single girl from out of town had called to ask if the organization knew of anyone who could host her for the night as she'd missed her bus home. The "*shidduch*" was arranged in no time. I called Mrs. Brody and told her I wouldn't be able to make it, but that I was sending someone else instead.

I took a month's break before starting my schedule of sleeping once a week at Mrs. Brody's. And when I did, I brought her a box of fresh, homemade oatmeal cookies to enjoy.

Esther Talks:
Believe It or Not

The cordless phone seemed to mock me from its perch on the coffee table. It had just been transformed from a trusty pal to a despised enemy. It had been the bearer of an ugly piece of information, a tidbit which every part of me wished wasn't true.

The wonderful memories of the past nine years, the fierce love that had pulsed in my heart, were reduced to a mound of rubble in ten short minutes. Collapsed. Destroyed. My friendship with Shevy was a thing of the past.

"You'll never believe what Shevy just told me," Miriam had said to me on the phone earlier.

Miriam wasn't whom I'd call my best friend, although she may have liked to consider herself so. She teetered on the fringes of the solid relationship that Shevy and I had built up between each other. Both Shevy and I shared a strong liking for Miriam, but we were equally loath to give up the "best friends" title we bore since our early days. And so we never actually formed a trio.

"Esther," Miriam had said, "I had a long talk with Shevy last night. She…told me…something you wouldn't like." Miriam paused for effect. "She said that she'd decided to give up her friendship with you."

Were my ears playing tricks? What was it that she was saying? I felt myself breathing in short gasps.

"Shevy told me that she thinks you're not really her type anymore. I just wanted to prepare you so that you aren't thrown off when you notice the sudden change in her…"

"Not her type anymore?" My head was whirling. I needed a drink, I needed a bed; I suddenly felt like a hapless victim of a horror incident. I was.

How could a metamorphosis like this be occurring? What had happened to Shevy and my age-old declaration that "we fit each other like hand and glove"?

I thought back to my last few dealings with Shevy. Come to think of it, maybe she *had* been treating me a bit more coolly lately…

Hard as it was to believe Miriam's words, it seemed they were true.

When the next morning dawned, the sun outside seemed far removed from me…as much as Shevy was. I felt like I was plunked in a thick fog. I buried myself under my covers and stayed there for the rest of the morning. I mumbled something about a headache to my worried mother; I'd decided to keep the issue to myself for now. I didn't want to pull my mother into the pool of anger and hurt.

Life had to go on. I reluctantly propelled myself to school the next day, but I studiously avoided Shevy's gaze and feigned nonchalance about the sudden end of our friendship. As the days passed, Miriam took my place as Shevy's best friend; she surely reveled in her new status. In the meantime, I searched for a new friend. But something in me resisted forming a new relationship. I missed Shevy so much...

Tests came and went, extra-curricular activities cropped up now and then, the annual class trip passed. Every experience made the hurt surface again. The ill feelings, like neglected weeds, grew rapidly. I felt a huge lump rise in my throat whenever I saw Shevy. The chasm between us enlarged and solidified.

Weeks turned into months, months into years. Yes, years. For two whole years, not a word was exchanged between us.

The application for high school arrived in the mailbox. I sat over the thick sheaf of papers, in a quandary. Who in the world would I fill in as choices for classmates? There was always Naomi, whom I was friendly with, and Sara, with whom I walked to school. But none of the relationships were what I'd call deep or close. I skipped that part of the application, hoping that things would somehow just work out.

And, unbelievably enough, they did.

Taking my place on the line for the standard interview with the high school principal, I suddenly noticed who was standing right ahead of me. Shevy. I instinctively turned my head away and pretended to be reading a notice on the bulletin board.

The wait was long. I managed to sneak a glance in Shevy's direction, and just then, she accidentally dropped her application booklet. As she bent down to pick it up, I caught a glance of the open booklet.

What I saw there changed the rest of my school years.

On the list of choices for classmates, I saw my name. *My name?* The black ink seemed to me a bright rainbow of color; the straight letters appeared to dance a little jig. She had listed me as her *first choice*?

I steadied myself to keep my composure. I discreetly flipped to page three of my own application booklet and scrawled in Shevy's name.

Shevy's eyes were following my every move. My face flushed a hot pink and I looked up. She did, too. And our eyes met.

Shevy took the first step. She called me that night. Seeing her name on the ID screen made my stomach do a big flip-flop.

"Esther?"

"Shevy?" I croaked.

"Thank you for choosing me to be your classmate," she said softly.

My throat went dry; I didn't know what to say.

"And...I...I don't know how all this happened two years ago. It was so sudden. I couldn't understand why it happened..."

What had she said? She didn't understand why it had happened? The conversation was taking an unexpected turn.

"*You couldn't understand why it happened?*" I didn't know

whether to be more angry or shocked.

"Well, one day we're the best of friends — and the next day you won't do as much as glance in my direction. That's as much as I know."

"Can we please be honest now?" I said, upset. "I'll try very hard to forgive, but please — don't play innocent now."

"Forgive? As far as I know, *I'm* the one who has to forgive. You left me so suddenly."

"Suddenly? After the whole speech you made to Miriam, how could I not leave you suddenly?"

"What are you talking about?"

Something was very strange.

I drew a deep breath. "Miriam told me you didn't want to be friends with me anymore."

There was a long silence on the other end of the line. Shevy must have been fighting back tears.

In a small voice, she said, "I said no such thing."

The silence stretched longer now.

The ugly reality stared me straight in the face.

I had been deceived, cheated, tricked. I had been robbed of my childhood friendship. Envy and gossip had been at play, and I had been the victim. Miriam had ruined two years of my life.

"But Esther, how could you have believed it?" Shevy said in an almost-whisper. "Didn't it occur to you that it might not be true?"

I was at a loss for words. Shevy was right. She was right for feeling betrayed. It suddenly occurred to me that *Shevy* had been deceived. She had been deceived by…me.

My furious thoughts suddenly changed direction. Instead of seething at Miriam, I became engulfed in anger...at myself. It was all *my* fault. *I* had been the one to ruin the friendship. *I* had believed the gossip and had ended the friendship. *I* was at fault.

✼ ✼ ✼

LIFE RESUMED as though the two vengeful years had never been. Shevy and I became closer than ever. As the expression goes, absence makes the heart grow fonder.

Miriam later begged both of us for forgiveness. She confessed to being consumed by an unquenchable envy. It was hard for her to always be on the sidelines of the close friendship Shevy and I shared. The gossip was her way of forming an undivided relationship with at least one of us.

We all spoke — Shevy, Miriam, and I. We expressed our emotions openly, and our talking had a tremendous healing effect on all of us. We learned that friendship with one person doesn't necessarily have to come at the expense of friendship with another; that we could — and *should* — cultivate other good relationships with other girls, without being afraid that our friendship with each other would be jeopardized. Friendship is not limited by any copyright laws.

Most of all, I was struck by the immense power of believing *rechilus*. When I had believed Miriam's words, it gave them the finishing touch. Her words only had an effect because I believed them.

At the start of high school, when everyone had to choose a learning program to join, I didn't have to deliberate much. *Shemiras halashon* was the way to go.

Devorah Talks:

Shabbos for Shoshana

When you say School Shabbos, you're telling me bliss. Our School Shabbos begins early Friday morning and ends late Motza'ei Shabbos. Friday's program includes: *davening*, breakfast, a *dvar Torah*, a comedy skit, a treasure hunt, a choir, challah baking, a snow fight, free time (a.k.a. more snow fights), showers, and finally *Kaballas Shabbos*. Friday night holds in store *davening* and singing, the *seudah*, workshops, and more singing and talking into the night. The agenda for Shabbos day is (starting from wake-up time, at about noon): *davening*, the *seudah*, singing, more workshops and debates, a game, free time (a.k.a.

schmoozing), *shalosh seudos*, a *kumzitz*, music and dancing on Motza'ei Shabbos, and a very late *melaveh malkah*.

I read and reread the schedule morning, afternoon, and night since the day we get it, until I know it by heart.

Finally, it is time. I am standing at the bus stop at six o'clock Friday morning, along with all the other girls, with a carefully packed carry-on suitcase and overstuffed nosh bag in tow.

Everyone is excited.

Except for one girl.

Shoshana.

Shoshana is standing at the far edge of the crowd, clutching her suitcase handle. She is not talking to anyone. She is not smiling. She is not laughing.

But nobody seems to notice.

Why should they? Shoshana is never part of things.

Shoshana is different. Shoshana has special needs. But she does not get special treatment, or any treatment at all. It's too easy to ignore Shoshana, and that's just what we do.

But I see Shoshana's forlorn face now, and I cannot ignore her. My heart won't let me look away. *Look at that face! Look at it screaming, 'I'm also a person; look at me, too!'*

Everyone is now climbing up the bus stairs. Shoshana follows the crowd. I watch her. She will not have whom to sit with. Our class has an odd number of girls, and she will for sure be the odd one out.

I walk on after Shoshana and watch her take a window seat, and promptly turn her face to look out the window. She has nothing — or no one — else to look at.

"Devorah! Devorah!" Gitty, my best friend, calls me from the back of the bus. "You don't hear me? I said, I have a seat for you here!"

Oh, no. What should I do?

"DEVORAH!"

I look at Gitty and then peek at Shoshana.

"Um, Gitty, I have a seat already."

"You have a seat? What do you mean? So why didn't you save one for me?"

What can I say? Should I scream across the bus, "Because Shoshana has no friends and she needs someone to sit near her"?

So I say nothing. Instead I sit down near Shoshana, and hope Gitty will see and understand.

Shoshana whirls around.

"Uh…is anyone sitting here?" I ask her.

"N-no."

"Oh, good."

I prop my nosh bag on my knees and settle down.

I am sitting near Shoshana. For a two-hour drive. No regrets.

I have to talk to her. Help! What should I say?

I say that I'm excited for the School Shabbos. She nods. I say that I had packed already by Tuesday night. She nods again and smiles uncertainly.

Now what?

I hear Gitty laughing hysterically from the back of the bus. A few girls join her. Soon the entire back of the bus is gasping helplessly with laughter.

And I am forcing a smile, and nodding, and forcing another smile.

I want to just get up and walk to the back of the bus. But…I also want to stay. Shoshana is really happy now. She is shining.

So I talk to her some more. I talk about the fun we will have; how funny the comedy skit will be, and how we'll sing ourselves hoarse at the *kumzitz*. We'll have a great time, I promise. We'll have a great time, Shoshana. Together. You and I.

Shoshana smiles, and I smile now for real. I've made her happy. And I can't wait to make her even happier.

The bus finally grinds to a halt on a bumpy, dusty country road, and finally, we are out in the fresh air. Ahhh…the magic of country air!

Everyone gets their luggage and starts sprinting to the bunkhouses. Off to the Bed Grab!

I walk into the bunkhouse and meet a whirlwind of activity. Carry-ons lie open on the floor, leaving almost no empty square foot there. Girls are dressing mattresses in colorful sheets, hanging up clothing in open wooden cubbies, and swapping candy bars. A CD player blasts music, and some girls break out in an impromptu dance.

Gitty is sitting on the bottom bunk at the end of the room. The bed on top is empty. And so is the top bed next to it. I break out in a run.

"This bed's saved for me!" I call out, throwing my nosh bag onto the bed on top of Gitty. "And this is for Shoshana!" I yell, loud enough for her to hear.

Gitty watches me quizzically. I return a huge smile to her, then to Shoshana, and then to myself.

DINI TALKS:

Surprise

My friend Lay-Lay's birthday was coming up, and Fay-Fay, Tov-Tov, and I were planning to make a mega celebration for her. It would be in my house right after school. We'd set everything up a day before — the balloons, the table, the treasure hunt — and my mother would just set out the food before we'd arrive. The plan was that I'd convince Lay-Lay to come to my house after school to see some pictures of my nephews. I knew she would first want to go home — she lived just a block away — and get her mother's permission. That would give everyone else enough time to race to my house, put on some silly Purim hats, and crouch near the door. As soon as Lay-Lay would knock, I'd turn the knob from inside and we'd pop up, yelling, "Surprise!"

We were getting underway with our preparations, cutting out letters for our "happy birthday" sign, when Tov-Tov suddenly said, "Oh, I totally forgot!" She clapped her hand on her forehead. "Naomi Kurtz will be staying at my house next week — right at the time of the birthday party!"

Oh, no.

Naomi was our classmate, and Tov-Tov's first cousin. Her parents were going to Israel for a week, and she'd be staying at Tov-Tov's house. But she was never part of our group of friends, and it would be really weird to have her at our private birthday party. Of course Naomi didn't know our secret code of nicknames, and we'd have to keep remembering to call each other by our real names.

"What should I do?" Tov-Tov pouted. "I can't run off to a birthday party and let Naomi go home by herself! I can't exactly tell her, 'You're cordially uninvited'!"

"Oh, boy!" Fay-Fay moaned. "After all our plans!"

"So let's be practical. We've got to think of an idea," I said, neglecting my half-cut "R" and sitting down on the couch.

"There goes Din-Din, practical as ever. So let's get thinking. Maybe…maybe you can ask some other cousin to invite her after school that day?" Fay-Fay suggested.

"Nah, we don't have other cousins our age."

"So…maybe, maybe we just have to push off the party!" I said.

"Aw, after all this? C'mon, Lay-Lay's getting suspicious already. We can't push it off anymore."

"So you'll just have to think of some excuse to tell Naomi," Fay-Fay said.

"You have a dentist appointment?"

"Or, you're getting a haircut and —"

"Hey," Tov-Tov interrupted. "You forgot we don't lie."

There was nothing to say. We sat quietly, thinking.

"This is a lost cause," Fay-Fay said glumly.

"Yeah, there's just nothing to do," I chimed in.

"Except one thing," Tov-Tov said suddenly.

Fay-Fay and I turned to her in surprise.

"We can invite Naomi."

"You must be kidding."

"We just can't —"

"But why not, really? Think about it. How much will it really ruin our party?" Tov-Tov challenged.

"We're a foursome since first grade!" Fay-Fay retorted. "It's us four and only us four. That's the way it always was!"

"So? We can invite someone else just once, can't we?"

No one answered.

Finally, Fay-Fay grumbled, "We can, and we can have a ruined party."

"Okay, complaints aside, this is our only option," Tov-Tov said briskly. "We're on!"

We finished cutting out the letters, but with less gusto than before.

Tov-Tov invited Naomi during recess on the day of the party. I couldn't help but keep a suspicious eye on her all day, wondering just how much she'd botch up our party.

During the break before our last history class, I asked Lay-Lay if she'd drop by after school to see some pictures of my nephews from England. As I'd expected — and hoped — she said she'd have to ask her mother. She'd go home first and then come to me.

The minute the dismissal bell rang, I packed up my things, my heart beating wildly. We had planned so much, and were really hoping things would go well. There would be just one glitch: we had an unwanted guest.

I strolled out of the school building with Lay-Lay like I always did, not wanting her to suspect anything. We walked together for most of the way, until we parted at my corner. Meanwhile, Fay-Fay and Tov-Tov — and Naomi — walked to my house through a side street. They were waiting outside for me when I arrived home.

We bounded up the stairs and burst through the front door. My mother had already set out the donuts, popcorn, chocolate mints, and drinks. The birthday cake would come out later.

We put on the multi-colored hats that we'd prepared before and ran to crouch behind the front door, laughing at each other on the way. Naomi straggled after us.

We crouched near the door, remaining absolutely silent. All we heard was the noise made by each other's breathing. After a few minutes of waiting, we got bored and started whispering excitedly.

Naomi was smiling shyly all along, not uttering a word. We felt a little bad, and I guess waiting near the door for way too long sort of forced us to be friendly to her.

Surprise

"Having fun, Naomi?" Fay-Fay started.

"Well, yes, but I guess this is just the beginning," Naomi stammered.

"You bet it will be a lot more fun," I assured her. "There'll be a treasure hunt, plenty of greasy, chocolaty donuts and other yummy nosh, and…"

"You forgot the out-of-this-world chocolate birthday cake!" Tov-Tov reminded me.

"Yeah, how did I forget *that*? We were up till eleven one night last week frosting and decorating it!"

"Sounds like you really worked hard," Naomi said, finally unfolding the arms that were clutching her chest.

"Sh!" Fay-Fay admonished. "I hear someone coming up the front stairs! I think she's coming!"

We held our breaths until we heard Lay-Lay's knock on the door. As planned, I opened it slowly, and then we all pounced on Lay-Lay, yelling, "Surprise!"

We blinked in the sudden flood of light, while Lay-Lay blinked in shock.

"Whoa! What a surprise!" She seemed at a loss for more words.

"We managed to pull it off!" Fay-Fay chortled. "And you had no idea, did you?"

"Nope, I didn't suspect a thing — though I have to say, you three *were* acting kind of weird lately, and I *was* wondering about that!" Lay-Lay laughed, but then suddenly stopped when she spotted Naomi for the first time. What was *she* doing here?

Tov-Tov caught on to her confusion. "Oh, Naomi's here with me. She's staying at my house for the week. We've been having a great time together so far."

Wow. I was impressed with Tov-Tov. She'd found the right words in the nick of time.

"Yes, Naomi, we're really glad you came," I hastily added.

Naomi blushed. "Well…thanks."

"Why don't we go peek at our spectacular birthday table?" Fay-Fay suggested, throwing off her yellow top hat.

I led my friends to the dining room. Streamers and balloons hung from the walls and ceilings, and the table spread looked mouthwatering. Lay-Lay's mouth flew open.

"Wow, what a birthday party! What a surprise!"

"Yup, you deserve it," I said.

"Okay, pals, if no one is thinking about the donuts, I will remind you all that I'm positively starved. Let's start with the FOOD!" Fay-Fay announced.

"Okay, poor hungry Fay-Fay. I'll give the donuts out. The birthday girl gets the custard doughnut, 'cuz we all know it's her favorite. Fay-Fay ordered jelly, so here you go. Tov-Tov wanted chocolate, of course, and she said Naomi likes custard, too. Is she right?" I asked Naomi.

Naomi nodded. I passed her the custard donut, and she flashed me a grateful smile.

As we munched on the donuts, Naomi cleared her throat and said, "Ummm…I also brought a treat for everyone." She reached for a bag under the table and pulled out four bars of milk chocolate. "One for each of you. A little way to say thanks."

"Oh, Naomi, you didn't have to!" Fay-Fay protested. "You'd be welcome without that, too!"

Naomi just blushed happily and handed out the chocolate bars.

As the treat melted in my mouth, I wondered if it was only the chocolate that made me feel sweet and good all over. I think that there was more to it. I was happy because I was having fun — yes, even with Naomi there — or maybe...especially *because* she was there? To me, that was the biggest surprise of all.

SARAH TALKS:

Teen Extreme

We met at the lunchroom sinks, and that was bad news. I had been examining my nails when Devora walked up near me to wash her hands for lunch. I quickly abandoned my nails and started for the door.

Devora stopped me. "Whassup, Sarah?" she asked. "You haven't washed yet, have you?"

My face grew hot. I wanted to get away from there as fast as I could.

"Oh, I was just examining this cut I got. Better get a band-aid." I left the sinks before Devora could say another word. I felt her staring at me, even with my face turned stubbornly away from her.

I walked as fast as I could, away from the confrontation. *Another* one.

They were happening more and more often, and I hated every one of them. Why couldn't everyone just keep to themselves? Couldn't I just act the way I pleased without people seeing and commenting on everything?

Or, perhaps, if I were honest, the question was really: *Couldn't I just be normal?*

I looked at my perfectly fine finger and wondered how I could have lied so easily. I guess I was more afraid of Devora discovering that I'd been inspecting my nails for a possible *chatzitzah* for ten whole minutes.

I never did wash my hands that day, and I went without lunch. There was just not enough time to wash my hands, eat, and *bentch* with real *kavanah* in a mere half hour.

My stomach rumbled hungrily during math, but I tried not to care. I was just trying to do the right thing, and if it was hard, I would only get more reward up in *Shamayim*, right?

✾ ✾ ✾

"So how is the new seating arrangement working out?" my mother asked me one day after I'd told her that our class had changed seats. "Is your class happy now?"

I was about to say that most of the girls were actually upset about the seating change, but I caught myself as a red flag in my mind suddenly warned: *Lashon hara!* I shouldn't be saying that my class was upset. That would reflect badly on my classmates, or maybe on my teacher who made the seating arrangement.

"Um…yeah, I don't know," I mumbled.

"Are you happy with your seat?"

I wasn't.

"Um…a little bit…I don't know."

My mother shot me a questioning look, but I offered no more. *Lashon hara* was a serious matter. Too bad if my weak responses cost me shame.

I went up to my room later, holding the cordless phone in my hand. I stared at it as if that could make it ring, but I had no such luck. It hadn't rung for me the whole evening, and practically the whole week, for that matter.

I fell onto my bed, burying the phone under my pillow. Yes, the phone days seemed to be buried, and I mourned them terribly.

Those long conference calls with my friends were over; the jokes and laughing were long gone. In fact, I couldn't remember the last time I had laughed.

Why did it have to be so hard? I felt the tears starting to come. I was only trying to do the right thing! Mrs. Kohn had taught us that a person was supposed to teach himself to be like a mute. Silence was a positive value.

Well, as far as my friends were concerned, if I kept quiet or tried cutting our conference calls short, there was no point in calling me anymore. I had nothing to say and was ruining all the fun; why bother?

There were times I wished I could be my old self, in the pre-Mrs. Kohn days, when I'd been the life of the party. Everyone had always known Sarah Stein as the fun, popular, and adventurous girl everyone wished to be friends with.

Until Mrs. Kohn came around. When Mrs. Kohn, our ninth grade *mechaneches*, walked into the classroom at the beginning of the year, I instantly knew that she was going to be my role model. Kind, honest, and warm, she was, to my mind, the ultimate *tzaddekes*. Her lessons were charged with spirituality; every single one of them left me with long-lasting inspiration.

I'd wanted so much to be like her. So I changed. Overnight.

❋ ❋ ❋

My sister and I were doing homework in our room, when she asked me if I minded handing her a pen. Responding with an instant yes, I passed it to her. Then I realized that answering yes might have been a lie. I *hadn't* minded handing it to her, right?

"I meant to say no," I immediately said aloud.

"What?" my sister called from the foot of the stairs. Oh, I hadn't realized she'd already left the room.

"I should have said no, that I *don't* mind handing you a pen."

"Sarah, are you okay?"

I wished I could yell that I really was *not* okay, and could someone please help me fast?

❋ ❋ ❋

Another time, my mother came home from a wedding and asked me if anyone had called.

"No," I replied, but just then the creeping doubt took hold of me again. Maybe somebody had called and the phone was busy. So I couldn't be one hundred percent sure that nobody had called.

"Actually, *maybe* no one called," I quickly corrected myself.

My mother looked confused. "Did someone call or not?"

"Um...I don't know. I mean, I didn't hear anyone call."

My mother looked at me strangely and shrugged.

There it goes again, I thought, feeling that very familiar pit in my stomach.

❊ ❊ ❊

"Shabbaton is here, Shabbaton is here!" The hall posters screamed in wild colors. Preparation was in full swing for the Shabbos that promised to be unforgettable. That is, for everyone except me.

I dreaded the upcoming Shabbaton. Shabbaton for me meant staying out of all the fun, and that would be really painful.

The mountains greeted us on Friday afternoon with cool, fresh air — a nice change from the stuffy, polluted city. I inhaled the scent of the trees and flowers, and felt invigorated by the growth around me. Somehow, I knew then that this Shabbos would be a nice time for me, for a change.

After the Friday night meal, I passed by a group of my classmates sitting and schmoozing in one of the bungalows. I overheard someone proposing a heart-to-heart "game." Every girl would have a turn to ask the others questions about what they thought of her. The girls took heartily to the idea.

I knew I had to join. This was my chance.

I took a seat in the circle, trying to avoid the curious looks darting my way.

The activity began. In the dark of the night, in the cozy Friday night atmosphere, honest opinions came out in the open. My classmates enjoyed the candid exchange; it was eye-opening, encouraging, and enlightening.

But most of all for me.

My turn came. My heart beat fast. There was a question I wanted to ask. But I was afraid to ask it — and even more afraid to hear the answer to it.

In a shaking voice, I asked, "What do you think of how I've been acting lately?"

An uncomfortable silence followed.

Then the answers came.

"Um…I hope you don't mind me telling you this…I mean, you asked, so I guess you want to hear…I think you changed a lot."

My heart beat faster. The truth was now being articulated into words. "Tell me, tell me everything."

My friends told me the truth. They saw me as extreme, fretful, and self-conscious. I was overdoing things.

"Sarah, we miss the old you. You used to be so much fun, always so happy… What happened to you?"

I felt like hugging every one of my friends right then. They really cared about me.

The tears came, first in trickles, then in torrents. With heaving shoulders, I let out all of my doubts, fears, and lack of confidence.

I told my friends how I hated covering up. I told them I didn't know how to get myself out of it.

My friends nodded and commiserated with me. They all agreed that I had to speak to someone about my problem and get some help; I couldn't continue on like this.

I felt awash with relief. I wasn't alone in my problem anymore.

And I knew just who I was going to speak to.

By the time we all straggled off to bed, it was in the wee hours of the night. I felt spent. But I was determined to become free from the prison I'd created around myself.

I approached Mrs. Kohn that Shabbos afternoon. Realizing that I wanted to discuss something personal, she offered to stroll with me on the country road near the camp we were staying in.

I spilled everything out again.

After I finished my piece, she smiled at me warmly and said, "Sarah, I want you to know that you're not the first person to go through what you're describing. These obsessive thoughts, the doubts that don't leave you alone...many times these are an indication of a condition called Obsessive Compulsive Disorder, or OCD. It's a condition that, with the proper help, is extremely curable. Believe me when I tell you that many people have had this condition — and have overcome it."

Wow, could that be? It felt so good to hear that I wasn't crazy; that other people had gone through the same torture as me and had come out on the other side, happy and normal once again!

"Sarah," Mrs. Kohn continued, "there's one thing you should always keep in mind. If you feel tense or anxious about life, something is going wrong. True *avodas Hashem* comes along with inner peace. If there's no inner peace, it's not *avodas Hashem*. I know you have the best of intentions. You're truly a special girl. But you need guidance to help you make your *avodas Hashem* real."

"Guidance?" I asked. "From who?"

"I'll be very frank with you, Sarah. You probably need guidance from a professional in order to properly work out this issue. These obsessive thoughts are dangerous to your emotional health. But I'm going to help you. Right after Shabbos, I am going to do some homework so I can give you the name of a competent therapist. I'd be happy to speak to your parents about it."

A therapist. I was both embarrassed and relieved.

Mrs. Kohn took my hand in hers. "Therapy is not as bad as it sounds. And you'll see what an amazing difference it can make in your life."

I believed Mrs. Kohn. "O-okay," I whispered.

Mrs. Kohn turned to head back to the camp, still holding my hand. "And Sarah, I'll also be there for you, to cheer you on and support you through the whole process. And eventually, when you'll feel happy inside, you'll know on your own that you're on the right track."

I felt a huge load roll off my chest. I wanted to thank my teacher properly, to let her know how much I appreciated her care and concern, but my voice choked up.

Mrs. Kohn just smiled her warm, inimitable smile at me, and I knew she understood.

It would take time until things would be good again. And I

would have to work hard, extremely hard, until I reached that point.

But thanks to Mrs. Kohn's encouraging words, I knew that the day would eventually come. I would smile again. I would laugh. I would have a life of happiness and true, joyful *avodas Hashem*.

Bracha Talks:
The Promise

It's that time of year again. One candle flickers at the window — it's the first day of Chanukah, the time of warmth, happiness, and gratitude. It's also the day marking a fifteen-year-old friendship pact...

* * *

YEHUDIS AND I had been best friends practically since we were babies. She was a spunky, happy-go-lucky girl who complemented my quiet nature perfectly. She was open and forthcoming — an easy candidate for a close relationship.

Our relationship was, indeed, close — closer than most friendships I knew of. We spent our spare time together and confided in each other about everything that was on our minds. There was nothing she didn't know about me, and nothing I didn't know about her. I knew everything about her family — too much, sometimes, I now believe. I could read her like a book. I could decipher her expressions any time, and could tell you what she was feeling just by seeing her face. We called each other "sissy," but we knew that friends could be closer than family.

When we were nine years old, we made ourselves a little Chanukah party. Yehudis always complained that her family never had Chanukah parties with their extended family, so we decided to make one on our own. We bought jelly doughnuts and chocolate coins, and played dreidel. We had fun trying to fry latkes until my mother came running down the stairs when she smelled oil burning.

In the height of our fun, Yehudis said solemnly, "You know, Bracha, let's promise that we will always make a Chanukah party together every year, for our whole life."

"'Kay, sissy," I said. But then I frowned. "Hey, but what about when we'll be married? How can we promise to make a Chanukah party then? Maybe we will even live in different cities!"

After a moment of thought, Yehudis said, "So you know what, once we finish school, we will at least call each other every Chanukah. I mean, we will call each other all the time, but Chanukah it's a promise."

I giggled. "Even when we'll be grandmas with gray hair, we'll still call each other!" We had a good time laughing and imagining ourselves in our old age.

Ideal as it was, our friendship, like any close relationship, had gone through its share of fights and arguments over the years — but it had always prevailed. We had always reconciled and reunited, like birds flying back to their natural habitat. Until we were in tenth grade.

Yehudis had begun befriending Shaina, an eleventh grader in a different school. They had started out as bus mates on the way to their respective schools, and ended up getting enmeshed in an intense — and dangerous — relationship. Yehudis was a pretty girl, and Shaina "helped" her dress up and look her "best." She led her into the world of nail polish, gelled hair, and beauty salons. Yehudis, curious and enchanted, followed Shaina reverently. She had always been at odds with her mother anyway, and this was another way to "do her own thing" and highlight her independence from her family.

The Yehudis I'd known had shrunk deep inside herself, and a different, defiant "Judy" had emerged. Our relationship continued — we were too close to separate — but the old Yehudis was becoming more and more obscured.

In the beginning, Yehudis even shared with me everything she did with Shaina, and I listened, not supporting, but not disapproving either. Not that my disapproval would have made much of a difference; Yehudis was trapped, and nothing I could have said would have changed that. I wished I could save her from this wild spiral into the abyss in some other way, but, in my immaturity, I was too afraid of risking our relationship to reach out and involve anyone.

Yehudis's spare time was now divided between Shaina and me. Once, I joined them on a trip to a mall. It was an act of denial, a desperate way to try to prove to myself that their relationship wasn't as destructive as I thought — but it showed me just the opposite. Shaina was a wounded soul from a dysfunctional family, and she was out to fight everyone — and did so with no conscience. She had lost her sense of right and wrong, and shame and dignity, and was heading full-force to a more "enlightened" lifestyle. And Yehudis was right at her heels.

After that trip to the mall, something inside me recoiled from the thought of continuing my relationship with Yehudis. This was no innocent child's play. Yehudis was in a bad place.

Throughout the summer following tenth grade, I agonized over what to do. I knew about the dangers of being friends with someone who's in the wrong crowd. I knew it posed a risk to my own *ruchniyus*. And the truth was, with Yehudis's infatuation in Shaina and all she represented, our friendship had naturally cooled off anyway. But…to officially drop the girl I'd been so close with for so long? Could I really go ahead and end our friendship, just like that?

I finally decided to contact a teacher I admired and ask her what to do. She told me what deep down I already knew: that for my own *ruchniyus's* sake, I had to end the relationship. But, she stressed, I needed to do it in a civil manner.

"Just because you reject the lifestyle she chose," Mrs. Bernstein explained, "you can't reject *her* as a person. You still have to show her the respect that every human being deserves. In your case, that would mean approaching her and explaining that though you are sad about leaving the relationship, you feel it is the right thing to do, so long as the situation with her other friend doesn't change."

I bit my lip. This kind of conversation would not be easy, to say the least.

"By talking to Yehudis about it and explaining yourself, instead of just dropping her without any kind of discussion, you're showing her that you still consider her a worthy human being, someone who deserves to be handled with sensitivity and respect. And Bracha," Mrs. Bernstein added softly, "keep *davening* for Yehudis. You never know whose *tefillos* will help Yehudis come back to her old self — and your close friendship — again..."

With a lot of trepidation, I approached Yehudis in person on one of the first days of eleventh grade and asked if she would join me for a walk. We left for the school courtyard and I drew a deep breath. I explained myself, and she listened quietly. She heard what I had to say, and understood why I was leaving our relationship. But as I'd assumed, she could not bring herself to go back to the old Yehudis at this point. And so, though we both ended our walk crying, we parted ways.

The last two years of high school were pleasant, but separate sailing for the two of us. We treated each other like we would any regular classmate. We could exchange a joke, share notes, but the close relationship was gone.

After twelfth grade, I didn't see or hear from Yehudis until I got married. She came to my wedding, we embraced warmly, and she even stayed for the dancing. But after that, we lost touch completely.

Every year when Chanukah came around — at first with me still in high school and then seminary; the next year as a newlywed; the year after that with my first daughter; and then the two years after that — I remembered my old pact with Yehudis and considered calling her. The truth was, I didn't know where Yehudis was up to in life, and I was a little scared to know. And it wasn't like she was keeping to our pact, either... She never called me.

But for some reason, this Chanukah, with my two little ones soundly asleep in bed and my husband's menorah glowing brightly for all to see, Mrs. Bernstein's words suddenly came back to me. She'd exhorted me to respect Yehudis as a person, no matter what spiritual state she was in. Showing a person respect could come in many forms, I knew, including...even a brief phone call. And deep down, I also knew that I should be honoring my promise. I've always prided myself in being an honest person.

Tonight, finally, I plan to give Yehudis a call. Who knows how much good may come from this single act? But regardless of all else, my reaching out to her tonight will be honoring my pact with her — and honoring my Torah obligation to love my fellow as myself.

Shani Talks:
Today Is Forever

Joy and pain hit me with a pang at the same time.

I sit at my graduation, surrounded by my dearest teachers and friends. School songs play in the background; classmates chatter excitedly. Cheesecake, bagels, and delicious spreads and salads are arranged beautifully on the table. Intense emotions charge the air: we are concluding an important era in our lives.

Inside, I cry.

As we sing our school anthem wistfully, arms over each other's shoulders, a stab of longing slices through me. Just yesterday I was still in school, an idealistic but carefree student. The world was mine, ours. We loved our school, we loved our teachers, and we loved our friends.

We were lucky, I know. Not all students are fortunate to have such a positive school experience. But for me and my friends, school was a close-knit family, where you felt accepted for who you were and respected for your ideals and dreams. The best of me came out in that beloved haven; there was the intellectual challenge, the emotional support, and lots of old-fashioned fun that made for a well-rounded school experience. I loved dissecting a Rashi, a Ramban, searching the commentaries to settle a paradox. I loved debating a *hashkafah* issue, plumbing it to its full depths, and finally emerging with the gleaming truth. I loved the earnest and mature conversations with my friends after school, the soul-searching till the wee hours of the night. I loved the private talks with teachers, asking questions and expressing my innermost feelings which I felt safe to disclose in that setting. I loved mastering biology and chemistry at a comprehensive level. I loved analyzing good literature, taking apart a sentence to discover its hidden layers of wisdom. I loved writing original compositions, weaving the strands of my creativity into an articulate piece. I loved school life.

But now it is all over.

And here I am, mourning my beloved high school years.

"Reminiscing" becomes the name of the game around the table of us graduates.

"Remember when we tried to hide from Mrs. Shoenberg in ninth grade for a Purim prank? We made so much noise that she found us in minutes!"

Everyone laughs.

"We were so full of ourselves then; who knew that one day we'd look back and realize we were just a bunch of overgrown babies!"

We laugh again.

"I remember trotting around in heels in ninth grade and feeling so proud of it when I visited elementary school!" Rochel giggles.

"And I was so proud that we could finally leave the room in the middle of class without asking for permission," Yochie adds.

"At least in the beginning, we didn't take advantage of that," Naomi says.

"Until we did. Remember the time we started walking out in the middle of algebra, one after the other, until there was half of the class at the water fountain?"

"Is algebra really over? I'm starting to miss it!" Hindy moans.

"Hey, Hindy!" Bina calls from the other end of the table. "Remember what you said when we studied for our last algebra test together? You said you'll have to make a *seudas hoda'ah* the day you can throw away that workbook! *Nu*...when's it happening?"

Mrs. Reichman, our beloved office secretary, passes our table and smiles.

"Reminiscing is fun, but it's also a little sad, isn't it?" She sits down at the head of the table. "Girls, I've lived a couple more years than all of you BIG alumnae" — she winks — "and I want to tell you something." Everyone leans forward to hear her words. "The past is special. Not because of what it was in itself — but rather, just because it *is* the past. The past is no longer challenging or difficult for us. There is no more tug-of-war or conflict. It is just a fascinating story for our review. It is like an interesting book you can read. So of course looking back will be special.

"But come on, girls, remember how you all once came storming into the office and complaining that midwinter vacation was too short? What a scene that was! You sure had guts!"

We laugh. We had planned that "petition" for two days.

"And now, I can see on a lot of your faces that you're wishing to be back in school, just one more time!"

Our laughter this time is a bit more restrained, as if it contains an element of thoughtfulness.

"Girls, we all miss the past," Mrs. Reichman says. "But remember, it remains forever; you can always re-visit it and reminisce. The past doesn't disappear. Everything you experienced becomes part of the beautiful book of your life. *But realize that the present will also soon turn into the past!* These moments that are currently happening will soon be moments you will ache for in years from now." Mrs. Reichman's warm gaze sweeps over us all. "So please, girls, learn from the gift of nostalgia — *and appreciate the present.* Make the most of it. Because one day, it will become the glorified past."

So it's not only high school that people reminisce about, I realize as Mrs. Reichman waves and moves on to schmooze with some mothers. *Everything* will slowly turn into that aching nostalgia. Even this moment.

"A penny for your thoughts." My friend Toby claps a hand on my shoulder. "I think we're thinking the same thing."

"Yeah, still pondering Mrs. Reichman's words."

Toby cups her hand in her chin and leans forward. "So."

"So…what do you say to a nice long walk tonight?"

Toby flashes me a smile. "I say that's a great idea."

And I smile right back at her. Another moment lived right, another beautiful memory that's been created!

RENA TALKS:
Within

Ever since I can remember, the "in" girls in my grade were my role models. Those girls with the long, high ponytails and thick-rimmed glasses were, to me, the epitome of self-confidence. So what if many times the things they chose to wear could not quite be described as *tznius*? These girls were *it*. If they sought to impress anyone, they sure succeeded with me.

Over the years, I chose friends with the trendiest skirts (okay, they usually happened to be the shortest skirts, too) and the coolest hairstyles.

All this was until I met Miss Mandel.

I walked into my ninth-grade classroom on the first day of school, shirt pressed and hair painstakingly styled. I snuck a peek at my friends. Yes, my shoes were quite similar to theirs, my skirt the right length. Phew, I made it.

Miss Mandel, our new *mechaneches*, walked in. A few minutes into the lesson, I knew one thing for certain: she was my new role model.

She won my immediate admiration. She somehow smacked of much more confidence than the well-dressed girls who made heads turn as they strutted down the hallways.

Miss Mandel's lessons had so much body, but also so much soul. She wanted us to experience her lessons on a deep level. She taught us Chumash, halachah, and *hashkafah*. Her *hashkafah* classes were my favorite by far, and I suspect they were hers, too. When she taught *hashkafah*, her soft words screamed with fire, with passion. Every one of her lessons came alive. They aroused all of my senses...and those of my classmates, too. The inspiration from those lessons didn't just stay on the blackboard — it *embraced* us.

Hilchos brachos were delightful tasting sessions, with plenty of culinary advice. Sometimes Miss Mandel schlepped an electric burner or toaster oven to school, so we could get hands-on experience with what different foods were made of and how that affected the *brachah*. Of course, we sat in a circle in the yard afterward and enjoyed a picnic with our very own creations.

She used every tactic to reach each of her students. She brought up thought-provoking discussions for the intellectually-inclined girls. The musical students were in charge of the tune and musical accompaniment to *Shiras Ha'azinu*. The artistic girls helped her decorate the classroom.

Everything about Miss Mandel said: "I care." Her devotion melted my teenage "don't-mix-into-my-affairs-I'm-fine-without-you" attitude. I left my pride behind and showed her open admiration.

I surprised myself by reading and rereading her worksheets at home. Yes, me, formerly shallow-minded Rena Hirsch! I couldn't wait for Miss Mandel's next lesson. A new world seemed to have opened up for me since that first day of ninth grade — the world of *ruchniyus*. *Mussar sefarim* began to inspire me; *mefarshim* in Chumash challenged me — for the first time, all of Torah seemed exciting to me.

And my old aspirations? They seemed to evaporate like snow on a sunny day. Who cared about the latest hairstyle? I was too busy enjoying the thrill of learning.

And then, an earthquake struck.

Miss Mandel got engaged. Yes, that was exciting and happy news, except that…she was getting married in two months. In Eretz Yisrael. And that's where she would be living after her marriage, too. Which meant that she would be leaving us…in just one more week.

One more week!

That week passed by with me in a daze. I couldn't believe that my beloved Miss Mandel would be leaving me. I didn't even care who'd take over for her; all that mattered was that Miss Mandel, my favorite teacher ever, wouldn't be teaching me anymore.

On Miss Mandel's last day of school, I shuffled to my seat, depression pulling me down, down, down. I saw Miss Mandel standing at the front of the room, about to give her farewell speech, but I was so enmeshed in my grief that I could hardly focus on her.

She started speaking, smiling and sad at the same time. Yes, she was leaving. She had to prepare for her wedding and her move to Israel afterward. But she wanted to ask us for one thing.

"Please, girls," Miss Mandel begged, and there were real tears in her eyes. "Don't leave these wonderful months and important lessons behind. I am leaving, but the world of *avodas Hashem* is not. Do keep searching, keep thinking, learning, and growing. Open the *mussar sefarim* we've learned, now, and later, and *much* later, after you leave school. Keep looking for opportunities to grow."

And then she said the words that shot straight into my heart: "Inspiration does not come from me. Inspiration is really within *you*."

Within me.

Then Miss Mandel left, along with promises to send us letters.

But her words continued to echo in my mind. *Inspiration is really within you... within you...within you...*

Within.

I felt a rush of adrenalin. I wanted to grow. If Miss Mandel — and this whole year up until now — had shown me anything, it was that I really *did* want to grow. I didn't want to stay shallow-minded and superficial, with my greatest thrill being the purchase of a new outfit.

And I could *still* grow, even without Miss Mandel's help. I might have to try harder than before, but spiritual growth was still very much within my reach!

Soon Miss Mandel's letters came, and we hung them on the class bulletin board. They were full of color, and joy, and encouragement. She reminded us of past lessons, repeating the powerful words she used to say. "Remember the purpose of creation: *Kol haneshamah tehallel Kah* — 'Every soul must praise Hashem'..." As I read her words, I tried to find them within myself.

The year eventually ended, and with it, Miss Mandel's correspondence. But she had left me with the greatest gift ever: the gift of knowing how to actualize my potential.

When I open a *mussar sefer* today, when I make a small step toward character refinement, Miss Mandel, wherever she now lives, deserves a standing ovation.

Tzippy Talks:
Wishes at the Window

"**Whose**" turn is it to go to Aunt Ida this morning?" my brother Ari asked over a morning bowl of cornflakes. "It's for sure not my turn," he hurriedly added. "I already went yesterday." He frowned dramatically.

Elisheva groaned. "And I hope it's not mine."

I chewed the last of my cornflakes and headed for the chart on the refrigerator. "Hmm...Monday morning, December 5th...uh-oh, it's my turn."

Now I had to rush. It was seven forty-five and I had to go across the street and run up the six flights to Aunt Ida's apartment, write down the list of groceries she needed, nod patiently for five minutes while she explained to me exactly what brand and what flavor she wanted for every item — just as she'd told me the week before, race down the steps, run to the corner grocery, grab all of the items (of course making sure to take the milk last), wait on the cashier's line, pay the bill, carry the bags back to Aunt Ida, heave them on her table, unpack the groceries, apologize that I couldn't exchange the bananas for riper ones because then I'd be late for school, zoom down the steps, race back to my house, grab my briefcase, and make it to the bus stop...all by eight thirty.

I knocked on the peeling brown door. Aunt Ida opened the door a crack and peeked out. Seeing it was me, she opened the door wider to allow me in. I eyed Aunt Ida, hoping to catch sight of a glint of a smile. There was none today. She swiveled her wheelchair backward so I could come in.

Luckily, Aunt Ida's apartment was always clean and neat. She had a cleaning woman every day. Her house was compact, with one bedroom, a small kitchen, and a tiny dining room, if you were able to call it one.

Poor Aunt Ida had been hurt badly in an accident as a teenager and had never walked since — at least that's what the neighbors said. And she'd never married. But if she wasn't a wife or a mother, at least she could be an aunt. She insisted that we call her "Aunt Ida," although she certainly was not our aunt, and felt proud to count us as her family.

Aunt Ida was wearing her gray bathrobe that morning. That wasn't a good sign. That meant that she'd just gotten up, probably because of some aches and pains, or because she hadn't sleep well at night.

"Good morning!" I tried to sound cheerful.

Aunt Ida just coughed in return. My heart sank. That meant I was in for a long talk on why she got a cold and what she took for it. I could repeat her talk by heart by now. Her window had been open a crack at night, or the heat hadn't been set high enough in the apartment. This morning she'd had cinnamon tea with lemon juice and some honey candies, but nothing seemed to be helping her feel any better...

Hoping to skip the talk, I got straight to business, pulling out a notepad and a pen to write down the grocery list.

"Okay, Tzippy," she started. "Get me a container of milk, but check for the latest date. And take it last. Two yogurts, plain and granola-flavored, cream cheese..."

As she spoke, I found myself gritting my teeth. Why did we have to shop for her *every day*? Ari had just gotten her groceries the day before. He could have bought her four yogurts, or ten, for that matter, to last her a week. We'd tried to hint to Aunt Ida more than once that we could do her shopping in bulk, like once in three days, or even once a week. That would save us a lot of time. But she was convinced that shopping every day assured her fresher food — although we knew that the grocery stocked only twice a week.

Aunt Ida began to slowly check her cabinets to see what else she might need from the grocery. I tapped my foot, feeling very impatient. I had to hurry. Couldn't she work more quickly?

Why did I have to do this altogether? Why did Mommy offer Aunt Ida our help? Aunt Ida didn't even appreciate it; all she ever had to give in return were complaints. Wasn't there a later date for the yogurts? Couldn't I find riper tomatoes? And didn't the almonds come in a bigger package?

I finished my purchase and hurried back to Aunt Ida's apartment. I checked my watch. It was 8:12. I really had to hurry. I prayed Aunt Ida wouldn't keep me long while she checked the groceries. But I made sure to seem calm and patient, because if I ever made the smallest move to the door before she finished checking the last of the items, she'd look at me sharply and say, "What makes you so itchy to leave today, Tzippy? Huh?"

I didn't want to get into *that* again.

Whenever I passed Aunt Ida's apartment building, I always made sure to walk quickly, hoping she wouldn't see me. Because when she did spot me from her window on the sixth floor — and she was almost always by that window — she'd call out to me and tell me to come up for a visit. And if it wasn't morning, Aunt Ida knew I wasn't in a rush, so she'd keep me there for a long time — a *very* long time. The visits ranged from a half hour to two hours or more. I couldn't even give the excuse that my mother needed me at home. She'd always call my mother to let her know I was there and asked her if she needed me. My mother, of course, always said that she let me stay, so I was stuck. I had to hear all about Aunt Ida's doctor appointments, look through her pictures for the hundredth time, listen to stories of how they washed laundry when she was young, and hear about how people are lazy these days.

Then she'd ask me tons of questions about school and my friends. Now, that wouldn't have been so bad, except that Aunt Ida kept on giving her advice and telling me her opinion about everything. Like, if I told her that I was studying with a friend for a test, she would tell me it was much better to study alone, and that studying with friends was a waste of time. I had to nod obediently, *or else*. That would have also been bearable, but then, when I'd come the next time, she'd ask me if I studied with my friend or not. When I'd reply that I actually had studied with a friend in the end (I couldn't lie), she'd call me a "frivolous youngster." Now what did *frivolous* mean? Didn't sound like a friendly word to me.

Sometimes she'd ask me to make her a tea. She'd sit in the living room and, while I was in the kitchen, she'd call out, "Tzippy! The kettle is whistling! Shut the flame!" As if I couldn't hear it myself. Then, "Tzippy! The sugar canister is empty! Open a new bag and refill it!" Like I couldn't see that myself.

At the end of those visits, I felt totally exhausted. All I wanted to do was plop onto my bed and stay there till the morning.

Before we had started the chart, Ari, Elisheva, and I had always argued over who had to visit Aunt Ida. We all had excuses: Ari had to study for a test, Elisheva was too tired, and I had homework to do. But in the end, someone had to give in. My mother wanted someone to visit Aunt Ida every day, either morning or afternoon. Aunt Ida was an unfortunate woman who'd suffered a lot in life, and my mother really felt bad for her. But still, did that mean that now *we* had to suffer?

Oh, well. There was no choice. My mother insisted on it.

After becoming sick and tired of arguing with my siblings every day about our Aunt Ida visits, I thought of the chart idea. I drew up a monthly chart, dividing up the visits between the three of us, and of course, making sure our turns were even. If someone went for an afternoon, that equaled two mornings, because it took double the time (if not more). But we couldn't only go in the mornings, because Aunt Ida wanted company during the afternoons, too... As you can tell, a lot of thought and logistics went into creating this chart, but it did at least make the "visiting Aunt Ida system" a bit more bearable for us.

One day I got a really bad case of the flu. The first thing that crossed my mind was: *Great, now I have an excuse not to visit Aunt Ida.*

But soon I saw it wasn't so much fun. My head throbbed so strongly, even with all the Tylenols and Motrin that I took. All day I lay in bed, sniffling, sneezing, and trying to sleep (unsuccessfully).

One day stretched into two; two, into three. During the day, the house was so quiet, with my mother and father at work and Ari and Elisheva in school. I felt bored and terribly lonely. I watched the clock all day, waiting for four o'clock. That's when everyone would come home and when my friends would call me or visit me.

Well, some friends did call, but *nobody* came by to visit. Day after day I waited for that *bikur cholim* visit — but it never came.

After a week, I was feeling a lot better, but still too weak to go back to school. At that point, when my friends still didn't come over for a visit, I started to feel resentful. Why didn't my friends come and visit me? It wasn't like I was contagious anymore; my flu was basically gone. And I didn't live so far from the school; in fact, my house was on most of my friends' way home.

At four o'clock every day, I planted myself near the window and watched my friends walking home from school. I saw Mindy, Chaya Rivka, and Leah; they were my best friends! Why didn't they care to visit me? They were talking and laughing; they seemed to have forgotten all about me. Hot tears rolled down my cheeks as I watched them walk further and further away.

The feeling of loneliness was worse than any headache or cough. My friends seemed to think it was enough to give me a call every two days or so. If only they knew how I wished they'd drop in and cheer me up a little after a long, lonely, quiet day. They just didn't know how I felt. They didn't realize how hard it is to be stuck in bed for more than a week with hardly any social interaction. And I had too much dignity to ask them to do a *chessed* and come visit me.

Finally, I felt back to myself again and was able to return to school. After a long first day back, I came home exhausted. I dropped my schoolbag on the floor and went straight for the fridge to get a snack. Suddenly, I spotted the chart hanging on the refrigerator door. A quick glance at it told me...it was my turn to visit Aunt Ida that day.

So feeling better meant back to normal — and back to Aunt Ida. I groaned. Now I had at least two hours ahead of me at Aunt Ida's. What a pain!

I quickly downed a cup of milk and some cookies. Then I headed for my room to do my homework. After a half hour of solving math problems, answering some history review questions, and studying for a spelling quiz, I got ready to go.

I slowly pulled on my coat and walked sluggishly out of the house. It was such a horrible feeling, going somewhere I really didn't want to go.

Nearing Aunt Ida's house, I spotted her peering out the window as she did every day. As soon as she noticed me, her eyes lit up and she waved enthusiastically.

Suddenly, I remembered myself waiting at my own window. I pictured myself peering out, hoping for visitors, as I had done just the day before. The feeling of loneliness rushed back to me. Again I felt the hurt, the hush of the empty house, the edginess and restlessness.

I felt what Aunt Ida felt.

I felt terrible for her. So that was how she felt *every day*?

Poor Aunt Ida.

I walked into the apartment building and spotted the old clock on the wall. It was five o'clock. I knew I wouldn't make it out of there before seven o'clock, but suddenly I didn't mind.

I thought about how I was making Aunt Ida's day, how I was brightening a lonely woman's life and making her just a bit happier.

Then I started bounding up the stairs, a genuine smile on my face.

Tirtzah Talks:
Reach for the Sun

I've always felt that in the summer, everything is sunny and yellow, happy, and promising. That's why I've always found the summer to be the best time to reach for the stars...and the sun.

One sun-drenched morning, Pessy and I sat on the brown steps at the back of our bunkhouse. We came equipped with pads of paper, pencils, and erasers. It was the day before Shivah Asar B'Tammuz. It was the time to reach up, to grow.

But how do you grow?

"Let's write down all the categories we want to work on." Pessy chewed the end of her pencil. "Then we'll write in a *kabbalah* that we want to take on in each category."

"Hmm. Sounds good. Everything on paper." I thought for a second. "But you know what — sometimes a *kabbalah* can be a little private. Let's make a rule that we don't have to share if we don't want to." I was already thinking of the *kabbalah* I'd have to make to stop fighting with my little brother Zevi day and night. I was a little embarrassed — a high school girl who still fought with her little brother.

"Sure thing. I'll even move to the opposite staircase so we won't mistakenly peek at each other's paper. Yell if you need help."

"Funny. But it *is* a good idea to give each other space for this. And we won't have to yell — it's not that far."

Pessy moved to the second step on the opposite staircase, just a few feet away from mine, and propped her pad on her knees. "Ready?"

I looked up at the sky. There it was — that bright, happy sun. *This will be great,* I thought to myself.

"So there's *shemiras halashon*, of course," Pessy started. I scribbled.

"And *ahavas Yisrael*..."

"And *chessed*..."

"What's the difference?"

"Well, *chessed* is actually helping others," Pessy philosophized. "And *ahavas Yisrael* is just having a good attitude toward others — you know, *ayin tovah* and all that."

I nodded. That was a good way of defining it.

"But being *dan l'kaf zechus* is still its own category. It's quite specific."

"Right." We had four categories already, and many more to go. The more, the merrier.

"There's *davening*, of course," Pessy continued.

"Let's divide it: Shacharis and Minchah."

"Fine. And category seven will be saying *brachos* with *kavanah*."

Yup. That was definitely on the *kabbalah* list.

"*Kibud av v'eim* is next, of course," I put in.

"And controlling anger…"

I bit my lip. That was a big one, but on the list it went.

"And being *b'simchah*…"

"And *zerizus*…"

We scribbled, and scribbled, and scribbled.

There were nineteen categories in all. Nineteen areas we needed to work on. It was exciting and foreboding all at once.

Now came the real part. I had to fill in a *kabbalah* for each of the nineteen areas. Just one small step in every area of my life, and I was on my way to becoming a better person.

"You can keep it private, but give me an idea when you have one, 'kay?" Pessy called out.

Shemiras halashon. This wouldn't be private. "For *shemiras halashon* I'm choosing an hour — you know what? Two hours — when I'll be careful not to speak *lashon hara*."

Pessy looked skeptical. She liked to be more creative. "But there are other ways, too," she said. "Remember Mrs. Stern told us that a person could also decide not to speak negatively about a specific person, or to change the topic when people are speaking *lashon hara*?"

"Right. Hmm — what should I choose?"

"Well, maybe choose a person who you often speak negatively about —"

"Like Mrs. —"

"That's already *lashon hara!*"

"Okay, okay, I was just joking! And I'm keeping my original *kabbalah* for this one."

So there it was, on paper: Kabbalah *number one: from four to six every afternoon I will,* bli neder, *not talk or listen to* lashon hara.

So far, so good.

For *chessed*: *I will help out at least two friends each day.*

For *ahavas Yisrael*: *From three to four each afternoon, I will be on the lookout to find at least one positive quality in the people who come my way.*

"Hey, Tirtzah, where ya up to?" Pessy was scribbling away as she spoke.

"*Ahavas Yisrael*. And you?"

"I'm up to *kibud av v'eim*. I have seven *kabbalos* already. Isn't that great?"

"Amazing. I could just see you being the next *rebbetzin* of the generation."

"Hah. So what's taking you so long? Need help?"

"Actually, yeah. What kind of *kabbalah* can I make for *dan l'kaf zechus*? It's a pretty hard thing to remember as it is."

"Right. So I wrote that I'd judge one person favorably each day during a conversation that I'm having with that person. When you're talking, it's much easier than when you're thinking, to realize that you're judging someone badly — and you can stop it and say out loud why the person might be right."

"I like that. Okay, I'll do that, too. Hey, can I be assistant *rebbetzin*?"

✼ ✼ ✼

I LAY ON THE TOP BUNK, my mind swirling. Tomorrow. Tomorrow was the first day I had to keep the nineteen *kabbalos* I undertook. Shivah Asar B'Tammuz seemed like the right day to start.

At night I dreamed of a gigantic, human-sized clock, with large, hammering hands going around and around the face, while I ran to the beat, trying to fulfill all of my *kabbalos*...

✼ ✼ ✼

PESSY AND I MET in the woods behind our bunkhouse right after breaking our fast. We'd arranged to do this "general progress report," as we called it, for the first week of our *kabbalos*, to check up on how we were doing with them.

"Ten," I said without introduction.

"Nine."

"Not bad, really not bad." Pessy sounded happy. "We did achieve something."

"I don't know. These were *kabbalos*, not just random things on a 'to-do' list. And it was Shivah Asar B'Tammuz today. How did I forget *nine kabbalos*? I didn't say *Hamotzi* with *kavanah*; I didn't give anyone a compliment today; I don't think I was *dan l'kaf zechus* anyone... I don't know. I think I'm giving up already."

"That's it? You're out? Come on, give it a fair try. It's a new day tomorrow. A new day, a new chance."

"Nice, nice, *rebbetzin*. Okay. One more try. But if I don't keep at least seventeen of my nineteen *kabbalos*, I'm out. Yup, it's all or nothing. This was a project, and if I fail, I fail."

"Okay, okay. Stop being such a pessimist. *My* name's Pessy, by the way."

The next morning might have been bright and sunny, but I woke up with a dark cloud over my head. Nineteen *kabbalos*. What was number one?

❈ ❈ ❈

That night I didn't even show up for our progress report. I forgot all about it. Pessy confronted me in bed, climbing the ladder of the bunk bed to face me squarely in the eye. If I wasn't so dejected, I would have laughed out loud.

"We had an appointment, Tirtzah."

I sat up with a start, and suddenly I was rambling. "Look, Pessy. This is not going to work. This is never going to work. I did not keep even *one single kabbalah* today. I even forgot we were supposed to meet tonight. Okay, maybe I wanted to forget. But I want to BREATHE! I *need* to breathe! I can't keep looking at my watch and trying to remember which of the nineteen *kabbalos* I'm supposed to be doing now. It's just too much. That's it. I'm done with it." My voice grew sad. "But how I'm ever going to get somewhere in *ruchniyus*, I have no idea."

I thought Pessy would look disappointed. Instead, she smiled.

"You won't believe it, Tirtz. I was just about to tell you the same thing. Except I remembered to show up tonight behind the bunkhouse."

Suddenly, we both laughed. Pessy was still suspended in mid-air, with one foot on the top rung of the bunk-bed ladder.

Pessy climbed onto my bed and sat near me. "Let's meet at our private spot anyway. We have to talk about this, Tirtz."

"I don't know, Pessy. Don't be insulted, but I'd rather wait for tomorrow night. Right now I just wanna rest and sleep it over." I felt all wound up, with nineteen coiled springs chasing around my brain.

For a change, I went to sleep at curfew. I had no strength for any late-night adventures or DMC's (surprise, surprise). Every bone in my body screamed: "Sleep!"

In the morning, I was almost convinced that I should go to bed on time every night. It was a long time since I'd felt so refreshed when *"Modeh Ani"* blasted through the camp loudspeaker.

Pessy and I met after night activity. I had my *kabbalah* papers in hand. I knew I had to do something about the whole business. Three pages of *kabbalos* was just not the way to go.

"Pessy, I have to get rid of this. These papers are not letting me breathe."

"But it's the Three Weeks, and we hear so much about taking on *kabbalos* and all...how can you say that?"

"I didn't say we won't do *anything*. But not this. Let's tear this up and start again, start something different."

"What?"

Usually Pessy was the one with the brainstorms, but suddenly, I knew just what to do.

"First of all, we choose *only one thing*. Only one *kabbalah*. If you choose two, you're out."

"Go on."

"It should be something that's really important to you, that you really want to work on and change."

Pessy was nodding her head.

"And it doesn't have to be numbers — a time of day, a number of times. Not everything works that way."

I chose to work on having a better relationship with my little brother Zevi, and I wanted to start right away. I ran to the payphones and called him at home to wish him a good night.

Zevi was delighted. And so was I.

Faigy Talks:
Comfort

Libby is my best friend. We have a private joke that we could read each other's mind, and we're so close that we really almost could.

Libby is as devoted to me as I am to her. She knows just what to say and just what to do, at just the right moment, to make me feel happy and cherished. And I try to act in the same way to her. I search for the right words and the right responses so she knows I am always there for her, too.

Until the day came when those "right words and right responses" eluded me.

Libby's mother had a baby, a beautiful little girl — but the baby's lungs unfortunately were not that beautiful. They had a serious defect, and, at just a couple weeks old, tiny Goldy had already undergone a number of operations.

Libby was stricken with fear. She already loved her precious, suffering sister to pieces and was petrified of what the future held in store for Goldy.

When Libby and I spoke, she cried. I guess you can't really call that speaking. She cried, and I fumbled for the right words — and never found them. How could I comfort her? How could I relieve her piercing, terrible pain?

I was afraid I couldn't.

Goldy was in a remote hospital, a two-hour distance from our community. Every Shabbos, from the day Goldy was born, Libby spent Shabbos in the hospital with her father and the baby. Her mother had to be home for the rest of the children, and so her father stayed with Goldy, but he needed Libby to be there with the baby whenever he had to go *daven*.

One day Libby begged me to come to the hospital with her to visit her sister. Inwardly, I recoiled — I couldn't stand to see pain or illness or imperfection. I couldn't bear seeing a baby connected to tubes and machines, or the faces of worried nurses and doctors.

But instead of acting like a coward and making up an excuse for why I couldn't come, I looked Libby in the eye and said, "Of course. When do you want to go?"

We took the train to the hospital that Sunday afternoon. The ride left us plenty of time for talking and soul-searching.

"You know, when you're in pain and everything's not all perfect, you appreciate everything in your life so much more," Libby said as she looked absently out the window. "Like my parents. My other brothers and sisters. My friends." She smiled and looked at me. "Suddenly it seems silly to complain, or fight, or just bother with nonsense. Know what I mean?"

I knew what she meant.

The train stopped right near the hospital. As we walked through the hospital's entrance doors, I looked around at the huge building and buzzing lobby and walkway. Were there so many people suffering? For a moment, I felt like running away.

But I was at Libby's side. And I had to stay there.

Goldy really was gorgeous. Behind the tangle of tubes were the most exquisite features and long, lush eyelashes. As I stared at her through the thick glass that separated her from us, tears jumped to my eyes and trickled down my face before I could do anything to stop them.

I looked at Libby. She was crying, too.

We opened our arms and hugged for a long minute.

Afterward, we sat down and ate the sandwiches we'd brought along. It felt sacrilegious to chatter about school, or play Boggle, in such a somber setting. I kept searching for the right words to say to Libby, but I found none. So instead of talking, we just sat there quietly next to each other. We *davened* Minchah, peeked some more at the baby, and said some Tehillim until it was time to go.

The next Motza'ei Shabbos, when Goldy was exactly ten weeks old, I got a phone call from Libby. When I answered the phone, all I heard were wrenching sobs.

And immediately, I knew what happened.

"I...I...can't believe it! How could it be? How? How? How could it be?" Those were Libby's only words in our twenty-minute phone conversation.

"Oh, Libby..." I could think of nothing else to say.

She cried, and I cried. She sobbed, and I sobbed. She sniffled, and I sniffled.

And then I knew that that was all Libby needed. I listened and I cried, and in a tiny way, I made things a little better for her.

Rivky Talks: Accepting

"**Who** wants noodles?"

"ME!" the unanimous cry comes from around the table.

I count again; I think I had made a mistake before. There's Shloimy, Sara'la, Liba, Naomi, Ari, Elchanan, Tzippy, Mendy, Shani, Chezky, Yochie…wait — who just slunk out of his seat? Oh, well, I lost track again.

Shani's mother places a huge bowl of noodles and tomato sauce in the middle of the table, and Naomi, the oldest, spoons some onto her plate and passes the bowl to Shloimy. Shloimy takes some noodles and passes the bowl on to Liba, who then passes it to Chezky, who passes it to Yochie, who passes it to Tzippy, who passes it to Ari, who passes it to Sara'la, who passes it to…

The bowl reaches my seat, and I take a spoonful before passing the bowl to Shani.

"Oh, come on, Rivky," Shani says. "You won't finish it — do you see the bottom of the bowl yet? And there's more in the pot, trust me!"

She turns the bowl and lets a string of noodles slide onto my plate. I chomp happily, smiling at all the slurping and chewing and chatting sounds around me. It's almost like eating in a class, except that here, there are no desks or monitors…or a bell ending all the fun. The fun goes on here all day long.

I turn around to peek into the kitchen and nearly gasp. The pots are…humongous; why, a *kid* could fit in there! Now Shani's mother is dishing chicken nuggets out of the middle-sized pot, which is bigger than any of the pots *my* mother uses at home.

"Probably takes your mother all day to cook these huge suppers," I tell Shani in between bites.

"Oh, but we all chip in. See that chart on the fridge? Everyone's got a job. Today, Chezky boiled the pasta, Liba breaded the nuggets, and Naomi sliced the zucchini. Good you came on a day I didn't have a dinner job."

"And the little kids? Do they have jobs too?"

"Sure — no one gets away with anything here! They mostly set the table and help clear off. Yochie's only five, but she sweeps after dinner some days! She does a pretty good job by now."

"A chart sounds like such fun. Can I have a job, too?"

Shani laughs. "You know how it is; one day it's fun and we're all working with music blasting and everything, and another day we're all yelling at each other and arguing about whose job is whose."

Can I tell you a secret? That kind of fighting sounds like fun, too.

Everyone's chattering around me, and I laugh at three-year-old Mendy's rendition of *"Modeh Ani,"* which he suddenly gets up to sing, and Tzippy and Elchanan's argument over who is taller. Well, it really is a close competition. Tzippy is nine and Elchanan is eight, and it's hard to tell who's taller.

I can't argue on that one with anyone in *my* family. My one and only brother is eight years older than me, and away in yeshivah for a few years already. I love when he comes home, but the rest of the year, which is most of it, I'm a one-man show.

I frown into my plate of chicken nuggets. Supper in my house is a quick, no-mess affair. My mother and I sip boiling soup in our quiet kitchen; my father only comes home later. Dinner is over in fifteen minutes tops, and then I have the whole long evening to myself. I grimace. Boooring.

But my thoughts about boring things disappear in a flash. The noise and clatter and fun catch my attention; nothing's boring around *here*. Naomi is entertaining the wide-eyed little ones with a story she heard in school, while Shani's mother plunks two trays of colorful ice cubes on the table.

"They're orange juice ice cubes," Shani offers and drops two cubes into my cup.

"What an idea."

"Yeah, it's like ices, just cheaper."

Cheaper. I didn't think of that. I do get ices pretty often, but for a family with this number of kids…

I try to smile. At least I get ices.

Eventually dinner is over, and Shani and I head for our textbooks. But we have trouble finding a place to study. The bedrooms are all strewn with toys or books or crayons and kids, and the living room sofa is taken.

"We gotta go to the basement," Shani grumbles. "But it's freezing there. Get your coat and I'll bring down our portable heater."

We hobble down the rickety steps leading to the black basement. Shani flicks on the light. It is quiet here. And cold.

But the warmth from the dinner table upstairs keeps me feeling comfortable. Once in a while, strains of happy playing waft down the stairs, and I smile. Those kids are so cute, and happy, and energetic…

"Wild," Shani says with a frown when I articulate my thoughts to her.

So what? That's part of the fun. I'll take it any day.

Can you believe I'm disappointed when we finish studying? Yup, I wish I can study here longer. I want to stay in this happy, lively house, just…just a little more.

❊ ❊ ❊

TODAY MY HOUSE is extra quiet, and I'm edgy. My mother is out at an appointment, my father is at the office as usual, and I am doodling hearts and stars on a piece of paper and feeling very sorry for myself.

It's not fair. If only I had a bigger family. If only our house was more lively. If only...

I rummage through the fridge and find some leftover chocolate pudding. Goody. At least there's something sweet to eat, if I have to eat alone.

I lick the last of the pudding and then wander to the bookcase. I pick up a book, but I can't concentrate on more than one paragraph. Ever heard of a problem focusing when it's quiet? Sounds weird, I know, but sometimes quiet is more disturbing than noise.

Music? I'm too grumpy now. You could say I'm too grumpy to get myself not to be grumpy.

Suddenly, there is a drop of envelopes at the front door. *Maybe I got a letter,* I think. *Yeah, right. That's what you wish when you're bored.*

But I have nothing better to do, so I skim through the insurance letters, bills, and catalogs...and I see IT. A letter from the camp office! I tear open the envelope.

Dear Rivky,

We are pleased to inform you of your acceptance to Camp Chaveiros. Attached are the medical and financial forms to be filled out and returned by March 5. We look forward to a spectacular summer together.

Camp Chaveiros, Administration

Yippee! Yes!

I'M ACCEPTED TO CAMP!

I dance a little jig, and then laugh at myself. Hooray — summer's coming up, and I'm accepted to camp!

I smooth out the forms on the kitchen table. I can't wait for my parents to come home and hear the good news.

A sudden thought strikes me. Will Shani's mother fill out these forms for her daughter, too? No, Shani doesn't go to camp.

Shani's parents can't afford to pay for camp for all their children, I know. So Shani stays home, in the steaming, sticky city all summer, and works as a day camp counselor to make some money.

Do I want that?

No.

But I want that lively, fun family. I want little sisters and brothers.

Uh, excuse me? Order, please. Six sisters and five brothers to go, minus the city in the summer.

Sorry, package deals provided only.

So I don't want to be Shani. Do I want to be me?

Now that's a good question.

Adina Talks:

Journey

My nose is pressed to the taxi cab's window as I watch the goings-on around me. People embrace each other; some cry, some pat children's backs, others walk to the airport gate, their heads turned as they wave.

The taxi door slams shut and my father wheels the suitcases through the airport's automatic doors. I run after him into the teeming airport. We're going, we're going...we're going places! This time it's Italy. Italy makes me think of pasta and tomato sauce. I love that. I bet my father will buy me plenty of it in far-off Italy.

But the fun won't end with the food. My father promised me

trips and tours; he'll somehow squeeze them in between his business appointments. But even the meetings are plenty of fun for me. Each one brings new people, new dress codes, new languages, new accents. What will the Italians be like?

Will they be like the prim and proper Englishmen? Or like the Frenchmen, who sound like they're singing when they're talking? Or like the tiny Chinese? Or will they be something else altogether?

Visiting a different country is like stepping into the middle of other people's conversations. Everything is so strange. Even the swings in the kiddy parks look different in foreign countries. And the shapes and sizes and colors of the buildings wherever you look…nothing is familiar. But that's what makes the visit to each country so much fun!

We travel through the night, but I don't sleep. I walk up and down the airplane aisles, peeking at the passengers — discreetly, I hope. I sit down for a break and listen to the banter of languages around me. I smile to myself. I'm in for a fascinating trip. Aren't I lucky my father makes most of his business trips during summer vacation, and that he takes me along with him for so many of them, too?

On my next curious stroll down the aisles, a tall stewardess with hair caught up in a huge clip passes me by. She gives me a wink. "Can't sleep?" she asks in perfect English, but with a very emphasized accent.

I blush. Did she notice my not-so-polite activity?

"Not really," I finally say.

"Are you excited to travel?"

I bob my head up and down. "Uh-huh. It's my first time visiting Italy," I add.

The stewardess smiles. "I hope you enjoy your visit...and your trip back home, too!"

I return the smile, but I'm not so sure about the second part. I'm sure I'll enjoy this visit, but the trip back home? That's actually quite depressing — back to the same old... back to the sticky New York summer... What's there to look forward to about *that*?

But I try not to think about that part. Now is the time to enjoy.

We land in Italy. Here the sun's out — nothing like our dreary New York mornings. We step into the airport and it says one thing: Italy! Everyone's talking Italy, walking Italy, eating Italy. Welcome!

My father may not know Italian, but he manages just fine wherever the airplane takes him. It's not his first time here. I wonder if there's any country he's never been to. He hands our passports to the clerk, beats the escalator with his two-step climbs, and schleps our luggage off the revolving belt like an old-timer. Nothing new here for him.

We step out of the airport into the warm Italian air. Strange-looking buses catch my eye first. The policemen in Italian uniforms; the women's hairstyles; the smell of tomato and basil; the Italian chatter all around. I almost forget to blink.

"Adina!" My father waves to me. He's already standing near a cab. Oh! I didn't realize he was waiting for me!

I watch the houses, people, and dogs (yes! Somehow even they look different!) fly by as we drive. Finally, we reach an impressive-looking, pale orange building with Italian flags waving from the windows.

The hotel is shiny and carpeted, depending upon where you look. It is all I'd dreamed of in a hotel. I think back to our hotels in Germany, Finland, and Japan. Then I'd been all gung-ho, snapping pictures, touring the place from top to bottom, sometimes peeking into the kitchen. But I'm getting smarter now. This hotel is the real stuff. Even the clerks look fancier here.

My father sends me to get our room key, and I clutch it proudly. We ride up a mirrored elevator (four profiles of myself, smiling at me) to the eighth floor. Room 805, here we come! The room is all pomp and glitter. The bedspreads, lamps, and curtains are gold, and the wall paint, furniture, and bed sheets are shades of burgundy. I tiptoe; I don't want to ruin this picture of royalty.

My father laughs. "Feel at home!" he tells me.

During my father's long business meetings, I tour the forty-story commercial buildings. I watch the view from thirty flights up until my head spins. Then I watch people coming in and out of offices, calling out in rapid Italian, and I even figure out some Italian words.

Later, my father takes me touring. Even when I'm tired, I feel like I could go on and on. The view is refreshingly different; the people are more fascinating than museum exhibits. When my father calls it a day, I reluctantly follow him into the hotel.

Our two days in Italy are the shortest two days I'd ever had.

It is time to pack up and leave. I take one last, longing glance at our gold and burgundy room and drag my feet into the elevator and out the hotel building.

❋ ❋ ❋

My mother knows what I'm thinking as I shuffle through the door with a halfhearted smile. She throws her arms over my shoulders and squeezes me tight. "Trip's over, huh, Adina?"

I nod tiredly. "Yeah…" Then I brighten. "Ma, when's Tatty going on another business trip? I can't wait for the next time!"

My mother chuckles. "Next time? First, chocolate chip cookies and some rest. After that…we'll see from there!"

Well, I can't balk at chocolate chip cookies, can I?

But it's not only chocolate chip cookies on the table. Near them, vanilla muffins stand neatly, with a small card propped against them that says, "Welcome back!" A cellophane-wrapped package rests near it. I study the transparent packaging: inside is a book, a Tehillim, and a diary. My mother sits down next to me. She has something to say.

"I want to tell you a little story, Adina."

I give her a quizzical look. A story? Now? But my mother is a great storyteller, and I am intrigued, so I lean forward expectantly and say, "Sure, Ma, I'm all ears."

My mother begins. "Deep in the forest, some leaves once decided to challenge a tree. 'Hey, tree!' they said boastfully. 'Your life is so boring. You always stand in one spot; you never get to visit other places. We, on the other hand, have an exciting life: we travel; we fly; we see new, interesting places.'

"The tree just shrugged. 'Oh, I'm not jealous,' he replied. 'I may stand in one spot, but that makes me strong. I have deep roots;

you can't move or shake me. I am strong, tall, and powerful. I have so much more value than you puny leaves! And after all your travels, what remains? You lay crumpled on the ground.'"

My mother puts her hand on my shoulder and lets the message sink in.

I sit there quietly, mulling over my mother's *mashal*. I think of myself, a fluttering leaf, flying, traveling, visiting exotic places around the globe. And I wonder if maybe, just maybe, I can be a tall, stalwart tree, happy to be in my place, with true, eternal value inside.

I finger my mother's gift to me, still pondering the gift of her words. I'm back home now...and now might be the perfect time to begin another journey — this time, the journey within.